THE BRITTANY MURDERS

An absolutely gripping cozy murder mystery

ANNE PENKETH

A Brittany Murder Mystery Book 1

Joffe Books, London
www.joffebooks.com

First published in Great Britain in 2023

© Anne Penketh 2023

This book is a work of fiction. Names, characters, businesses, organizations, places and events are either the product of the author's imagination or are used fictitiously. Any resemblance to actual persons, living or dead, events or locales is entirely coincidental.
The spelling used is British English except where fidelity to the author's rendering of accent or dialect supersedes this. The right of Anne Penketh to be identified as author of this work has been asserted in accordance with the Copyright, Designs and Patents Act 1988.

Cover art by Jarmila Takač

ISBN: 978-1-83526-325-9

For Brigitte and Michel

CHAPTER 1: A PARTY

It was 3.20 a.m. and Jennifer was dreaming about food.

She picked up a steaming mug of builder's brew and inhaled its robust aroma. In front of her was a slice of moist carrot cake. She scraped off a strip of the buttercream icing with her finger and licked it off with the tip of her tongue. It was the most delicious thing she'd ever tasted, her favourite comfort food. She picked up a knife to cut into the cake, which was placed on a granite counter. When she turned and looked up, she saw railings and the feet of a man and a woman walking along the pavement. At that very moment of realisation that she was back in their basement kitchen in London, the knife sliced into her ring finger just as a long shriek pierced the air.

Jennifer rolled over as the sound travelled through the open window. She felt unsettled, not knowing why she'd woken. Something wasn't right. She blinked, staring up at the ceiling while she adjusted to the dark. Then her gaze fell onto the familiar shapes of the bedroom furniture, the chunky wardrobe that they'd bought in a local *brocante* and the heavy chest of drawers that had almost defeated their attempts to get it up the stairs. She switched on the bedside lamp to check that her finger was still intact. Jonathan grunted beside her and turned towards the darkness.

She lay there, hardly breathing, attentive to the slightest sound. She listened for footsteps on the wooden staircase. In this remote part of Brittany her fear of a night-time intruder kept bubbling up. She knew it was irrational but couldn't help it. Were the children still safely tucked up in bed?

She looked across at Jonathan's back, his lean body curled away from her under the duvet. The nights were cool in late September and he'd taken to wearing a crumpled T-shirt and boxer shorts. She had on her winter pyjamas which Jonathan had once described as "unsexy". She'd retorted that they were comfortable, which he seemed to have taken to mean "no sex please, we're British". If it was a strategy, it was working. She sat up on the edge of the bed and picked up her slippers. As she creeped to the door, another ghostly cry rang out from outside. It sounded human. Could it be a neighbour's child in distress at this time of night? The nearest house was half a mile away.

She moved to the window and pulled open the curtains gently, so as not to wake Jonathan. She knew what he'd say. The risk of anything happening to them was far greater in Hackney than here in the middle of nowhere. Peering into the darkness, she saw a white shape swooping over the hedge. The screeching had only been from a barn owl on the hunt. She drew the curtains again and slipped between the bedsheets.

She shut her eyes tight, willing herself to get back to sleep. This time she was thinking of a different type of food. She began mentally drafting her shopping list for the next evening's pantomime "reveal" by the couple who ran the village amateur dramatic society.

Jennifer and Jonathan were expecting eight guests at their *apéritif* for the event. She felt excited because at last they'd been invited to join the Louennec players by Craig and Meredith, the troupe's founders and self-styled leaders of their small expat community.

She and Jonathan had agreed that taking part in this year's panto would not only be fun but would also help them integrate. They slightly envied Craig's status of village elder as an elected councillor of their *commune*, particularly as they were still trying to work out the social pecking order.

"It's like being initiated into the Freemasons," she'd said to Jonathan, pulling a face and curling her fingers on top of her head in a weird Masonic gesture.

So, with her thoughts turning to crisp baguettes, and counting France's two hundred and sixty-five varieties of cheese instead of sheep, she drifted back to sleep.

* * *

Pippa was the first to show up for the party, holding a tin of homemade biscuits. She was the most recent arrival in the village and had made friends with Jennifer at the market where they both had stalls. Jennifer sold produce from their market garden, while Pippa still had the naive enthusiasm of a new arrival, convinced that the Bretons would flock to try her curries.

"Am I too early?" she said. "Sorry, I didn't see any other cars outside."

Jennifer thanked her for the biscuits and wiped her hands on her apron. "Don't worry, the others will be here in a few minutes. I asked Craig if I could invite you, and he said the more the merrier. You'll see, it will be fun." She turned her back before adding, "Jonathan can take care of things while I show you our little empire."

She led Pippa along a grassy track to the farthest end of the smallholding, past a barn and a couple of stone outhouses where tools and machinery were stored. Banks of roses, dahlias and hydrangeas were in bloom along a fence. "The rabbit hutches are in there," she said, as they passed the barn.

They reached a pasture where a black-headed ram stood behind an iron gate, staring at them balefully. A strand of hay hung from his mouth.

"He looks vicious," Pippa commented.

"He is. I think the ewes are afraid of him. They're probably in the shed. We're hoping to have lambs next spring."

Jennifer smiled. "The children will like that. They call him Rambo. I can't imagine why."

Pippa took another look at the sheep. "Great balls of fire," she said.

"Exactly." They giggled.

Jennifer turned and they began to walk back towards the house, a white stucco building whose front bedroom windows poked through the slate roof. She showed Pippa the rows of lettuce and haricots verts in the vegetable patch and a plastic greenhouse covering festoons of tomatoes, noting with pride, "It's all organic, of course." A fruit tree heavy with white peaches spread out beside the greenhouse.

A small table with a couple of rickety chairs, shaded by a grubby yellow parasol, had been installed beside a pond full of weed. "This started out as a goldfish pond after we got here last year," Jennifer explained. "But I don't know how many are still there, because I've seen a heron who seems to like helping himself. I keep asking Jonathan to put wire netting over it, but I'm still waiting."

She checked her watch. "We should get back."

Pippa noticed a wooden henhouse down a slope behind a wire fence.

"We've got a dozen hens in there, and a rather noisy cock," said Jennifer. "And up there" — she pointed to a coop in a field on the other side of the track — "we keep the broilers that I sell at the market."

Jennifer waved to an older couple who were opening the front gate.

"That's Craig and Meredith. He's the panto director, and she writes the script." She lowered her voice. "You'll see, he always gives himself the best roles."

Meredith followed her bearded, stocky husband as he strode down the path. Her long grey hair, loose-fitting cotton dress and sandals gave her the look of an Earth Mother.

"How many are you expecting tonight?" Pippa asked. "I don't suppose I'll know anyone."

"There'll be ten of us, including you," said Jennifer. "I think Craig wants to hand out the roles tonight, and then we'll have the first read-through next month. You know Adam, don't you? He's the estate agent who sold us the house."

"Oh yes. I bought mine from him too. That's good."

Jennifer did the introductions.

"Greetings, Pippa," Craig boomed. "Welcome to Louennec." Jennifer took them in through the front door framed by wisteria and ushered them into the kitchen where Jonathan didn't seem all that pleased to have been abandoned. He was bent over a tray of food on the granite counter, Byron, their golden retriever, sitting at his feet on the stone floor. The counter was the only thing they'd splashed out on since moving to the village. The kitchen still had the wooden 1960s units that they'd not got round to replacing, and the white paint on the walls was scuffed. A couple of drawings of trees and matchstick men were pinned on a board next to some family photos.

"Do you remember Pippa?" Jennifer cast her apron aside. "My friend from the market."

"Yes, hi Pippa. Come through, come through, everyone," Jonathan said. He lowered his voice. "So, Craig, tell us the name of the panto before the others get here. Don't keep us in suspense."

Craig shook his Old Testament beard. "All in good time," he replied so that everyone would hear.

They heard the front door knocker. Pippa felt the anticipation mounting as Jonathan shooed them into the garden where chairs had been arranged in a horseshoe shape for the event.

Nobody could have imagined that by the end of the evening, one of the guests would be dead.

CHAPTER 2: THE "REVEAL"

The party had got off to a convivial start, despite Craig taking charge as everyone had expected.

He and Meredith settled in at the top end. Craig had made straight for a deckchair, whose canvas folds curved around him, and his bottom almost touched the ground. He was trapped like Gulliver. He lit a cigarette while waiting for the others, blowing smoke rings into the air.

Pippa found a wooden chair at the far end of the group. As she sat down, the other guests filed out of the kitchen, followed by Jonathan who handed out the drinks. He had the local Gros Plant white wine in one hand and a bottle of red in the other.

The first was a young man with pointed city shoes and bleached blond hair shaped into a quiff. He could have stepped straight out of an ad for a Greek island cruise. Pippa immediately recognised Adam who had found her house in a quiet cul-de-sac in the village centre. Behind him was a gym-toned man in his fifties holding the hand of his younger trophy wife, and an unsmiling middle-aged man with a paunch.

Jennifer also emerged from the kitchen and observed their little group as they each found a chair.

"I want you all to meet Pippa, who's joining us for the first time," she said.

Pippa waved from her seat. "Hi everyone, I'm Pippa. Or Peeper, as the French call me. Thank you for inviting me."

"She's a brave woman who thinks she can overturn centuries of history and persuade the French to buy baguettes from a Brit," Jennifer explained.

"Well, good luck with that," Meredith commented. "In Carhaix?"

"No, here in Louennec," Pippa replied. "I thought they could do with a local *boulangerie*, so I've leased a place opposite the church. In the meantime I've got a market stall which you might have seen, and I'm doing a crash bakery course in Rennes." She smiled. "I guess I'm an eternal optimist."

"There aren't many of those in this country," said Craig.

"I've never understood why there's no village bakery," said Meredith. "We could certainly do with one."

"I don't recall hearing about your plans," said Craig. "You spoke to the mayor's office, did you?"

Pippa was about to respond but Jennifer was already cracking on to the next guest. She noted that Adam needed no introduction. "I think probably most of us here bought our properties from you." His smile displayed a set of dazzling white teeth.

Jennifer moved on to the gym bunny and his wife, perched like a sparrow on the edge of her seat. Derek wrote the songs for the panto and played the piano, she told Pippa.

"He's a doctor turned fitness instructor, and Solenn is a jewellery designer," she added. Pippa noted the heavy silver pendant on a chain round the neck of the thin woman.

"Bienvenue, Solenn," said Craig. "Another first-timer joining the players."

Solenn glanced at her husband, who gave her an encouraging wink.

"And last, but not least, this is Mark," Jennifer continued. "If you need help doing your French taxes, he's your man."

Mark waved in acknowledgement but didn't look up from the glass of wine he was pouring for himself. Pippa wondered if a dark stain on his pullover was from his last meal.

"Is that everyone?" Jennifer said. "There's an empty chair next to Pippa."

Craig replied, "Emma's coming, but she might be a bit late. She had to close the store tonight before checking on Romy." He added, for Pippa's benefit, "Emma's our daughter and Romy's our granddaughter."

"Should we start without her?"

"You're the hosts." Craig shrugged and picked up his briefcase which contained a sheaf of papers. The mystery Christmas panto would soon be revealed.

"Right then," Jennifer said to Jonathan. "Let's get the nibbles." And they headed back inside.

A glamorous brunette in her late twenties then appeared down the side of the house, dressed in tight jeans and a white shirt under a black leather jacket. She seemed flustered.

"Sorry I'm late," she said. Her lipstick was scarlet. "Busy day." She waved to the group, saying "Hi, Mum and Dad" to Craig and Meredith, before making her way to the empty chair where she introduced herself to Pippa.

Jennifer and Jonathan returned, each holding a tray laden with baguettes cut into squares spread with pâté and *rillettes*. Jennifer caught sight of Emma and offered her a drink.

"That's fine, I can get my own," she replied, getting up.

"Help yourself, the glasses are in the living room, behind the table." Jennifer's eyes narrowed as she noticed Jonathan offload his tray quickly before following Emma inside.

"Bring out some more wine, would you?" she called out. "Then we can get started."

She paused before adding, "Just one sec. I've left the cornichons inside. Does anyone need anything else? Anyone cold? I can bring out a shawl or a blanket."

The guests smiled, their mouths full, shaking their heads. Jennifer went inside and opened the fridge. She could hear low voices in the living room. If they were talking about the school run, why did they need to whisper?

"Jonathan, Emma, Craig's just going to start with the explanations, are you coming out?" she called out. A few minutes later they were all assembled. Jonathan offered everyone another round before leaving the empty bottles on the grass beside his seat. Mark poured himself another glass from the bottle by his side.

"OK, take it away, Craig," Jonathan commanded.

Craig stroked his beard and stubbed out his cigarette on his paper plate, which he placed on the grass, and leaned down to take out the papers from his briefcase. He seemed to be wondering whether to stand up for his presentation, but he was more comfortable sitting down. He tried to sit up straight, but the deckchair canvas pulled him down.

"Ladies and gentlemen, this year's pantomime by the Louennec players will be — Mother Goose!" he announced.

"Aah," they said in unison. Jennifer was disappointed. Aladdin was her favourite but nobody had been allowed to make suggestions. In any case, Craig would have cast himself as Widow Twanky.

Solenn seemed to be thinking, *What is it with these Brits?*

"I see you look puzzled, Solenn," Craig said. "Let me explain the story. Mother Goose is poor and threatened with being evicted from her home by the village squire. She's a very kind person but she's ugly. Along comes Priscilla the Goose who lays golden eggs which is *eggs-tremely* good news for her." Everyone groaned except Solenn. "Shall I go on?"

"Dad will turn it into a pun machine, as usual," Emma said to Pippa, rolling her eyes.

Craig continued. "The evil Demon King offers Mother Goose a deal — he promises to make her beautiful in return for taking Priscilla. Mother Goose agrees to go to the pool of eternal youth, and sacrifices Priscilla — her best friend. However, when she returns from the magic pool everyone notices that now she's beautiful she has turned nasty. To cut a long story short, in our version Mother Goose realises that to save Priscilla she must kill the Demon King, after which she becomes kind-hearted again. So, the moral of the story is — money can't buy you love."

"Can't buy me lur-urve," sang Derek.

"Thank you, Derek. Anyway, I should add that Mother Goose, the main character, is always played by a pantomime dame," Craig went on.

Solenn leaned over to Derek who gave her a whispered explanation. Her eyes widened and she shook her head in disbelief.

"A transvestite?" she asked.

"Yes, a drag queen. It doesn't sound very politically correct, I know. But it's fun," said Pippa.

"So, Solenn, you've obviously never seen a pantomime before?" Craig asked.

"I thought they were for children," she said. Everyone laughed.

"Given the number of double entendres, they're for all ages. But luckily the innuendoes sail over the children's heads. At least they're supposed to," said Craig. "Don't worry, you'll get the hang of it."

"I presume you're going to be the villain," said Jonathan.

"The Demon King? Of course," said Craig. "That's becoming a bit of a tradition, isn't it? Unless someone else wants the role?" Nobody spoke. Jennifer looked at Jonathan, who winked.

"In the script that Meredith has just finished, there are eight main characters. We were wondering whether you wanted to discuss the roles tonight?"

"We'd better get it sorted out," said Jennifer. "I guess we'll have to do the first read-through at the next meeting."

"Correct," said Craig.

"Excuse me, Craig, so you're the Demon King, and also the director?" said Pippa. A couple of the guests smirked.

"It's only a small role. So, there's no problem with doubling up."

"And what about Priscilla? Does she have a speaking role? She sounds like fun," said Jennifer.

"She quacks, basically. It's a comic role," said Craig. "But look, maybe we should start with Mother Goose. Any gents here fancy dressing up?"

"I'll do it," said Adam, raising a tanned arm under neatly rolled up shirtsleeves.

Craig made a note. "Great. Now what about Priscilla?"

Pippa held up her hand. "I'd like to try, if that's OK. I won't have any problem learning my lines if all I have to do is quack."

Craig nodded. "Fine. Thank you, Pippa."

"Excuse me," said Derek. "I don't believe that geese quack. And Priscilla isn't a duck."

Craig wiped his forehead. "And what noise do they make, exactly?"

"They honk."

"Fine. I would simply point out that this is a pantomime, it's supposed to be funny, and I think a quacking Priscilla will be much funnier than a honking one. Does anyone disagree?"

Nobody dared. By the time they finished, having managed to agree on the small parts, it was dark. A glow from lanterns strung along the fence created a cosy and magical atmosphere.

Adam's phone rang. He held it up with a gesture and disappeared inside to take the call.

"If Derek is playing the piano, am I needed to turn the pages?" Solenn asked.

"No, no, I don't think so," said Craig. "But don't worry we'll find something for you to do."

Solenn looked at her husband before replying. "I've never done acting. And I don't know about this pantomime. It's *l'humour britannique*, I think."

"Actually, I was rather hoping that, given your artistic bent, you might organise some costumes too."

"Costumes? There are costumes?" Solenn asked.

"But of course. Mother Goose's dress for example. It has to be colourful and eccentric. Meredith can show you some examples, can't you, dear?" Craig said to his wife. Solenn seemed to have given up all attempts to understand what was going on.

"That's it then. We'll do the read-through in a week or so at ours," said Craig. He closed his folder and stuffed it back inside his briefcase.

The guests got up to leave. Jonathan and Jennifer were waving people off at the gate as Pippa came out carrying her empty biscuit tin.

"Whose is that car?" she said, pointing at a Renault sitting in the drive. "I thought I was the last out."

"I thought you were too," said Jennifer. "That's Adam's."

The three of them looked at each other, puzzled, before Jonathan said, "I'll go back in and check. I've not seen him since he took that phone call. I wondered why he didn't come back out to say goodbye."

Jennifer and Pippa waited by the gate. "I enjoyed this evening," said Pippa. "It cheered me up to meet some locals."

Jennifer laughed. "Craig's not everyone's cup of tea, as you can see, but he wasn't too much of a pain tonight. Honestly, the way he bosses everyone around you'd think he was the editor of the *Daily Mail*, not a retired sub-editor from the provinces."

The porch light came on and Jonathan returned with three torches. He was frowning.

"I can't find Adam anywhere," he said. "I don't want to wake the children by shouting his name. You two look on the right of the track over there, and I'll do the left. He can't have just disappeared into thin air."

Jennifer and Pippa advanced slowly in silence in the cool air of the late summer night. The sky was heavy with stars.

"It's so quiet here," said Pippa.

"Shh," said Jennifer, raising a finger to her lips. They heard a sudden screech and Pippa jumped. "What was that?" she whispered.

"That's the barn owl. He still frightens me too. With a bit of luck we'll see him swoop over the lane. He hunts in the field opposite."

They stood still for a moment but saw nothing so they carried on walking, swinging the torches from side to side as they searched in the darkness.

They reached the fish pond. Pippa gasped and grabbed Jennifer's arm. They recognised Adam from his pink shirt and white jeans. He was lying very still, spreadeagled in the water which glistened in the torchlight. His face was turned to one side, a goldfish was poking out of his mouth, its tail wriggling in its death throes.

CHAPTER 3: JENNIFER

Jennifer glanced past her line of customers, waiting to be served, to Pippa who was staring enviously at a queue of people in front of another market stall selling crêpes.

"Fancy a coffee when we're finished?" Jennifer called out. "I'm packing up in a few minutes."

Her customers were the usual combination of expats and tourists who stopped to buy and chat with her in English. The first category wanted to know about the dead body in her garden, while the second had come to explore the misty forests of Arthurian legend and the region's Gallo-Roman and Neolithic sites. That morning she'd had quite a success with bunches of dahlias in addition to her vegetables, chickens and eggs.

She felt sorry for Pippa standing alone at her curry stall. She watched as Pippa called out to a couple inspecting the food from a distance before shaking their heads and moving on to the charcuterie stall heaving with pâtés and saucissons.

"I like this place," said Jennifer as they pulled up plastic seats on the terrace of the Central Café, a stone's throw away, a few minutes later. "It's a bit down at heel compared to the other places round the square, but it feels authentic." She gestured towards the bar where locals were standing, drinking glasses of wine.

"There's Philippe from the market. Did you try his cheese?" She waved at a tall man in his thirties, wearing a leather jacket and jeans, who was looking in their direction. He smiled and waved back.

Pippa shook her head. She seemed preoccupied. The waiter brought over two coffees balanced on a tray, and she drew hers towards her to take a long sip.

"Never mind, it's early days," said Jennifer. "It'll take a bit of time until they get used to seeing you selling curry. I bet you end up with regular customers like me."

Pippa pulled a face. "I know. But why on earth did I think I could sell biryani to the Bretons? I mean, I'm a businesswoman and I did all my market research. I identified a gap in the market, and let's face it, mine is the only one here. But what is it with the Bretons? Why aren't they more adventurous?"

"I know," said Jennifer. "They eat couscous, don't they? So they like spicy food. I guess curries just aren't part of their culture, yet."

Pippa grinned. "Frankly I can't wait to branch out with croissants and cakes, now that I've started my bakery course. Maybe I can pull them in gently that way, until I open my bakery."

"How's the course going? I've sold all my eggs today but if you want to pop round in the morning I can give you some fresh ones."

Pippa smiled for the first time. "Oh thank you. It's pretty tiring actually. I have to leave the house at 6.30 every morning to get to Rennes in time."

"Well, your French is good. That's a big start."

"Yes, luckily. I used to work for a French bank in the City, and obviously French was required."

Jennifer looked impressed. "I see. So you're not short of a bob or two, then!"

Pippa smiled. "Well, I got a payoff, actually, a couple of years ago. The bottom line is that I was overlooked for promotion and took out a discrimination case."

"And you won?"

"Yes. There was a clear pattern of promotion of male, French managers where I worked. There's still an incredibly macho culture in the finance industry. But I realised that I'd never be able to work again in an investment bank. It's the sort of thing that sticks to your reputation like mud. People think you must be a troublemaker."

Jennifer nodded in sympathy.

"So that's why you decided to move here?"

"Exactly. What about you?"

"We're OK thanks to Jonathan's financial consultancy work," Jennifer replied. "My contribution is pocket money really. But we share the outdoor work, thank goodness."

"And what brought you here, then?"

"It was Jonathan's idea really. He wanted to get out of the rat race in the City. As I was freelancing as a photographer, it was easier for me. I had schoolgirl French, and his wasn't much better, but our main concern was how the kids would adapt. We thought Luke would be fine which he is, and in fact his French is better than any of ours now. And Mariam was eleven and about to start secondary school, so we decided to take the leap."

"And has it worked out?"

Jennifer's eyes clouded over and she lowered her head. "It's hard to tell. She's become a different person in the year that we've been here."

She didn't know Pippa well enough to admit that she was at a loss. They'd hoped that Mariam would flourish in a bilingual English and French class in Carhaix, but in fact she'd withdrawn, particularly over the last few months. Her teachers said she was "finding it difficult to adjust", which Jennifer took to mean that her daughter was being shunned by her classmates. Mariam, a naturally curious and intelligent child, looked different from the three other pupils from England in her class who were white and from rural areas back home. She'd still never brought any of her classmates to the house.

Every time Jennifer asked about whether everything was all right at school, Mariam always looked her straight in the eye and replied, "Yes, why?" in a tone of voice that caused her to back off immediately. Was she a victim of racism? It hadn't been an issue in Hackney, where their daughter had mixed with the white, brown and black members of her class indiscriminately. These days, she spent most of her spare time upstairs on the computer, like most kids her age. But who was she communicating with? "Friends," Mariam retorted, when asked.

Pippa broke into her thoughts. "How old was Mariam when you adopted her?"

"She was only a few months old. She's originally from Somalia, but with the civil war going on she ended up in a refugee camp in Kenya, near the border. To be honest, we don't even know if she was taken there by her birth mother because of all the chaos." Jennifer paused, and took a breath. It was a long time since she'd spoken to anyone about this.

"Anyway, that's when the two of us were looking to adopt a child internationally. We were just about to give up when we were contacted by a Kenyan orphanage. Mariam had been left by the side of the road outside the camp."

Pippa's eyes widened in disbelief. "On the side of a road? How awful," she said.

"Yes. Who knows what had happened to her in her short little life before she was abandoned."

Pippa shook her head in sympathy. "And does Mariam know all this?"

"No. We told her of course that I'm not her real mummy, and that she's from a country called Somalia in Africa. But not those details, no. How could we?"

They both stared into their coffee for a moment, and Jennifer licked the froth from her café crème.

"Did you get called in to the *gendarmerie* about Adam last weekend?" Pippa asked.

Jennifer's features darkened as she remembered the dead body found on their property.

"Oh yes. Although we couldn't really help, apart from saying that he never came out again after taking that phone call. The police were there until after midnight, and they said they were going to do toxicology tests. I suppose they don't know if he was on drugs, which might explain why he fell."

"Do you think he was? I mean, I thought he was lovely and really good at his job. In fact, I ended up buying the second house he showed me. But then of course I didn't know him socially."

"Neither did we, apart from viewing the property, but I liked him. He was very outgoing, like a typical estate agent, I suppose," Jennifer replied. "We had to give the police details of everyone who was at the party."

"I had to give a statement as well." Pippa frowned. "What if he was pushed though?" she added.

"It's scary, isn't it? I suppose nothing's ruled out yet," said Jennifer. "And we had to tell the children of course that the fish pond is off limits. It's got police tape round it."

She looked down at her watch. "Look, I'd better get going, they'll be wondering where I am."

CHAPTER 4: PIPPA

Pippa pulled into her driveway and fished in her handbag for her door keys.

It was really time to get to grips with the front garden, she thought. The cream-painted, slate-roofed house in her cul-de-sac was part of a new development in the centre of Louennec, and she hadn't yet had time to sort out the flowerbed. She took out the remains of the vegetable curry and carried it carefully into the kitchen. She hung up her jacket and sat at the table, her shoulders hunched. She felt defeated. She wasn't going to survive on a couple of hundred euros from the market every week. The rest of the weekend stretched in front of her like a life sentence. She brushed away a tear that had formed in the corner of one eye. What was the point of self-pity? She should have thought of this before leaving London.

She couldn't bear having curry *again* for lunch, and put the market leftovers in the fridge before making herself a sandwich. Then she took out her phone and Facetimed one of her daughters, rearranging her features to be resolutely cheerful. But Joanne was out shopping and promised to call back later.

She remembered that she'd left a bag of vegetables in the car and went outside. At that moment, her French neighbour turned his Peugeot into his drive. They greeted each other and he came over to shake her hand.

"*Ça va?*"

"*Oui, très bien merci,*" she replied. Her smile felt forced. "You're not working today?" she asked in French.

"Even gendarmes are allowed a day off from time to time," he said with a disarming smile. She examined him more closely. His military-style buzz cut suited him, drawing attention to his smooth skin and restless dark eyes. She caught herself wondering whether he might be slightly younger than she was, or maybe the years had been kinder to him. His figure was trim in a pair of jeans and a dark jumper. He'd need to be fit to chase down thieves, she thought.

"I was just going to make a cup of tea," she said. "Would you like one?"

"Oh you English and your tea. But yes, thank you," he said. "I'm Yann, by the way."

"Pippa."

"Give me a few minutes, I have some shopping in the boot," he said.

She heard the doorbell just as the kettle was boiling. "I feel like I live here," he said as he stepped into the hall. "It is identical to mine."

"Of course it is," she said. She noticed he was holding out a packet of biscuits.

"*Galettes bretonnes,*" he said by way of explanation. "For the tea."

She thanked him and put some on a plate before making the tea. He noticed a pile of drawings on the kitchen table.

"Did you do these? You're an artist?" He picked up the top one depicting a spreading oak tree, its branches bare. A child with big round eyes peeked out from behind the trunk. "Is this your child?"

This was starting to feel like an interrogation. She laughed. "No, my children are grown. I noticed that little boy watching me as I drew, but I'd never seen him before. I was in Epping Forest, in east London."

"Oh." His eyes moved to the fridge, where she'd put family photos on the door, her daughters larking about doing stupid poses in the country and at the seaside.

"Are you Breton, then, with a name like Yann?" she asked. She carried over two mugs of tea and invited him to sit down.

"Do you mean Breton *bretonnant*?" She'd never heard that expression before. He explained that it meant the Bretons who spoke the language fluently. "No," he said. "This part of Brittany is *bretonnant* but my family is from Rennes."

"Oh, I see. I've noticed all the signs are in French and Breton round here. Including at the supermarket," she replied. "But I'm wondering whether I made a mistake by moving to the country rather than somewhere like Rennes. It would be more like London."

"Ah, but London is huge compared to Rennes." They laughed.

"Your French is very good by the way," he said.

"Ah well, I worked for a French investment bank, you see."

"So, what brings you to Louennec?" he asked. He peered over his mug, his eyes sharp. The fingers clasping the mug were long and neatly manicured. "Le Brexit?"

"Not really. Well, only partly. And thanks to Brexit the paperwork was a challenge. Let's just say it was a work/life balance thing," she said, waving one hand. "I needed to get away. Start a new life."

She could tell he wanted to know more.

"You are here alone? No family?"

"No, it's just me. My two daughters are in Manchester, where they're both at university," she replied. "May I?"

She reached out for a biscuit. He smiled. She took a buttery bite before asking, "And you? Are your family with you?"

"I don't have children. I divorced some time ago. In this job it's hard because of the hours we work. And I've moved around the country. I only came back to Brittany about two years ago."

"So that's two years you've been here in Louennec?"

"I live here, yes, but my brigade is in Carhaix."

"Your brigade?" she asked. "Oh yes. You're military, aren't you?"

"That's right. I see you know France well."

"Well enough to know that you don't spend all your time handing out speeding tickets," she said.

He smiled. "In rural areas, we have a big role, it's true. If there's a car accident, we investigate. If there's a demonstration, we are there for security . . ."

"And murders?"

"Do we investigate murders? Yes, of course. Around here it's mostly domestic," he said. "But very few, luckily . . ."

"Are you investigating the murder of the British estate agent?" Her question prompted another piercing look.

"Do you think it was a murder?" he asked. "He may have tripped and fallen in the pond."

"Do you think so?"

He shook his head. "It seems unlikely, to be honest. Did you know him?"

Pippa nodded. "He sold me this house. What do you think? Was he killed because he was an estate agent?"

"Why do you say that?" He seemed genuinely curious.

"Well, in England, estate agents are right at the bottom of the popularity ratings along with journalists. People don't trust them, apparently."

"Really? I don't think we have such ratings here," he said with a smile. "But our Forensics have a lot of work to do on this case. Maybe his phone will talk to us."

"But wasn't it in the pond?"

"Yes." Pippa could tell that he didn't want to discuss it further.

"The investigation is just beginning," Yann added. He helped himself to another biscuit. "It seems he was a popular person. It will take time to interview people who can help us with the investigation." He finished the *galette* before asking, "And what do you do?"

"At the moment I have a stall on the market, selling curry."

"Curry?" His lips curled with amusement.

She added, "But I'm actually going to set up a *boulangerie* here in Louennec."

"Ah, what a good idea. I will be your best customer," he said. "Is it the empty store opposite the church?"

"That's right. I'm fundraising to renovate the store, and to help me buy the equipment."

She began ticking off the names in French, having already committed the vocabulary to memory. "I'd never even heard of a proofing chamber until I started this course."

"What is it?"

"It's a huge unit like a fridge with shelves inside, where you leave your dough to ferment. And you can set the temperature, and timing like an alarm."

"Impressive," he said. "It wasn't like that in the old days."

"I can only imagine. But it's made the baker's job a lot easier." Pippa went on to explain about the bureaucratic hurdles. "I'm afraid I hadn't realised just how complicated it was going to be," she said. "Madame Le Goff at the *mairie* put me straight on that. I don't think she likes me." As she spoke she was beginning to feel sorry for herself again.

"I wouldn't worry about her. She's a busybody." Yann waved a hand in the air dismissively. "But you do need a qualification, don't you?"

"Of course. I'm taking classes in Rennes. And then I have to work in a bakery for three months before taking my final exams."

"Bravo!" he said. "But you know the hours are worse than mine?"

"Yes," she replied. "They say that a baker doesn't have a life. But I'd had a desk job for so many years that I decided to do something completely different."

"Something completely different in a completely different country . . . You're a brave woman, Peeper." He put down his mug and looked at his watch. "I'm sure you have plenty to do this afternoon," he said.

Not really. "Thank you for the biscuits," she said, standing up. She accompanied him to the front door. Should she invite him back for a meal? she wondered. But before she could formulate the question, Yann had stepped outside, wishing her a "*bon après-midi*". He hadn't suggested a further meeting. Why would he? They were neighbours after all. She smoothed down her baggy jumper over her jeans and went upstairs to make the bed.

She felt weary. It had been a tough week at the cookery course where, at forty-three, she was one of the oldest in the group. She'd noticed the smirks directed at her from the youngsters half her age.

After shaking out the duvet on the bed, she couldn't resist stretching out on top of it. The lack of sleep had carved deep shadows under her eyes. She shut them and massaged her face, smoothing the beginnings of a double chin between a finger and thumb. *Why did I come here?* she asked herself again. *Because I needed to escape and reinvent myself.* That's how she'd come up with the idea of opening a bakery. But why here? She hadn't thought it through properly, she knew that now. She'd always thrived on a challenge, but why had she picked a small village where she didn't know a soul? Her daughters thought she was mad.

She swung her feet round and sat up, before saying out loud "*putain*". It was one of those catch-all expressions that beautifully encapsulated a range of feelings from astonishment to frustration and anger. She said it again, pushing her lips forward, then laughed.

She went back downstairs, her mood lifted, to clear away the kitchen table and decide what she'd bake with the eggs that she'd pick up from Jennifer the next morning.

CHAPTER 5: A NIGHT VISITOR

It was Jennifer's turn to feed the animals.

The breakfast table was already laid for Luke and Mariam when she creeped downstairs in a thick dressing gown over her pyjamas. Byron gave her a long mournful look and struggled to his feet. By now, their ageing retriever was a vet's bill on legs. As she made herself some coffee she could hear his loud slurping behind her. She pulled on her rubber boots by the front door, and scraped the soles on the wet grass outside to get rid of the mud.

She ventured out into the damp. Byron sniffed the air before deciding to wait outside the front door. She heaved bundles of hay into the sheep pen, before giving clean water, grain and a handful of hay to the caged rabbits. The broiler chickens heard her and began clamouring to be let out. She replenished their water and left them barley before going down to the henhouse, her last stop. She sprinkled a bucket of food waste in the coop for the laying hens who never turned up their beaks at anything.

But as soon as she opened the henhouse door, held shut by a single latch and hook, she stopped dead. The cock pushed past her into the chicken run, crowing hysterically. But where were the hens? Normally they trailed behind her while she filled up their water container. Glancing inside, she saw piles of bloodstained feathers inside and gasped.

What had happened?

She glanced into the corner where the survivor hens were cowering, clucking quietly, crushed together in the far corner. Then, she ran back towards the house, where she interrupted the children's breakfast of tartines. Luke was waving the butter knife in the air like a conductor while Mariam sipped coffee from a French *bol* which the children now preferred to mugs.

"What's happened, Mum?" he asked, sensing the excitement. Before Jennifer had time to respond, both children were out of the back door.

"Don't you go in the henhouse," she shouted, running after them.

"Get your father," she instructed Luke. Jennifer stood guard outside the chicken run with Mariam, who allowed her to put an arm around her shoulder before twisting away, until Jonathan emerged in his nightwear and wellies. They watched him push aside a couple of grey *cendrée* hens who were emerging through the half-open henhouse door before he disappeared inside.

He came out, shaking his head.

"What do you think?" Jennifer asked.

"I'll need some bin bags," he said, heading back to the house. She waited, motionless, until he returned and disappeared again inside the henhouse.

After about fifteen minutes, he re-emerged, carrying a bin bag in each hand.

"Four of them are dead, I'm afraid," he said. "But the *cendrées* were spared."

Jennifer sighed. Thank goodness, she thought. They were her favourites, and good layers.

"Shall I tidy up in there?" she asked. "I didn't have time to collect any of the eggs." Most of the survivors were now in the coop and were picking at the lettuce leaves and other leftovers that she'd thrown onto the ground, as though nothing had happened.

"Leave it to me," he said, walking up the slope to dispose of the bodies. "I'll deal with it later. I'm playing golf with Derek this morning."

Jennifer collected the breakfast things from the table while the others got dressed upstairs. But instead of tackling the washing-up, she stood at the sink staring blankly at the garden. She couldn't get the sight of the bloodied, dead chickens out of her mind.

The sound of a car door slamming made her jump. Who could this be so early in the morning? Perhaps the murderer returning to the scene of the crime? She went to the front door and screwed up her eyes to peer through the peephole.

"Oh Pippa, I'm so glad to see you!" She'd completely forgotten about the eggs.

Pippa looked perplexed, noticing that she was still in her dressing gown. "Aren't you *eggs-pecting* me?"

Jennifer laughed. "It's just that something terrible happened last night. I'm completely stressed out. Come in."

They went into the kitchen where they sat at the table. Pippa frowned when Jennifer explained about the night-time attack.

"I'd take you out to see the damage, but frankly I can't bear it. Months of effort gone in one night!"

"Could it be an animal that got in? Isn't that the obvious explanation?"

Jennifer shook her head. "Don't you think it's too much of a coincidence so soon after Adam was murdered in our own garden? I've never heard about an attack like this. We had a fox in the henhouse once, not long after we got here last year, and Jonathan saw him going off with a chicken in his mouth. We had to fox proof the henhouse after that. But this was like a Mafia hit. Completely different. I mean there's blood and feathers all over the place."

"So, what do you think? Is it a warning? A hate crime?" said Pippa. "A mad person from the village?"

"It's targeted, isn't it? I mean it's someone who's deliberately targeting our livelihood."

"A competitor?"

"Surely not," said Jennifer. "We've only got a little smallholding." She poured them both a cup of coffee.

"A bunny boiler?"

Jennifer laughed. "I don't think Jonathan has a mistress, if that's what you mean. Honestly, I've no idea who'd do this."

"Do you think it's because you're foreigners? Like Adam?"

She'd struck home. They looked at each other with alarm.

"Could well be," said Jennifer, slowly. They heard someone coming down the wooden staircase and Jonathan came in. He smiled at Pippa and waved.

"I'm off then," he said, closing the kitchen door behind him.

"Talk of the devil," Jennifer murmured with a grin.

"Look, I'll let you get on with your day," said Pippa, standing up. "What have you got on apart from solving the henhouse massacre?"

"Did I tell you I do some work for the local rag, *Le Télégramme*?"

Pippa nodded.

"I've got to take pictures of a farmer who's using facial recognition to keep track of his pigs."

"Wow. That's hi tech."

"Yes, but I'll have to rush to make it in time for the deadline, as I've got to stay in with the kids this morning." Jennifer got up. "Give me one sec, and I'll fetch you some eggs from the cellar."

* * *

It was almost lunchtime before Jennifer saw Jonathan again. She'd gone round with the hoover to suck up the dog hairs on the sofa, shaken Byron's blanket outside and mopped the kitchen's stone floors. They couldn't afford a cleaner anymore. Back at her observation post from behind the sink, she gazed into the garden which stretched down to a row of lime trees behind the hedge. Her eyes were drawn to the fresh mound of soil outside the kitchen window. Soon, the grass would be ruined by molehills. Had Jonathan noticed the new lumps pushing up like a gigantic tumour?

Her thoughts returned to her conversation with Pippa. Was it possible that Jonathan had a mistress? Amid all the stresses and strains of their new life, they'd become Jennifer and Jonathan, even to each other. They'd never discussed it but they were no longer Jen and Jon. Was it so long ago that they'd been a double act like Bonnie and Clyde or Sonny and Cher? These days they spent so little time together, with Jonathan shut in his office under the eaves while she took care of the smallholding. He might have the incentive to stray, but between their work and shared child care duties, when would he have the opportunity?

She heard the front door click and his approaching footsteps, the familiar clunk of wellies on stone. She bit her tongue before she was tempted to say, wipe your feet. Byron, stretched out beside her, lifted his head and stirred his tail.

"Where are the kids?" he asked as a greeting, pulling up a chair at the table.

"Upstairs. The last time I checked, Luke was reading Harry Potter and Mariam was on the phone."

"I fixed it." Jonathan had always been a man of few words. It was a trait that had only begun to irritate her with the passing of time. "I cleaned up inside and repaired the cracks. That should do it."

"Good. Thanks." Jennifer sat down next to him. Jonathan stretched out a hand towards her.

"Look, I know you're upset about this, but shit happens, and we'd better get used to it," he said. "We knew that when we left London."

"But who do you think could have done this?" she asked. "I mean a deliberate attack on our earnings?"

"What do you mean? It was a weasel of course."

"How do you *know* that?" She was starting to feel uncomfortable. She didn't dare mention the theories she and Pippa had aired because she knew exactly how he'd react. She'd been so certain that the intruder must have been human. It was only natural, after what had happened to Adam, wasn't it?

"Google," he said. "They're killing machines. They can get through the tiniest crack. It's always a bite to the neck, and the victims bleed to death."

Then he muttered, almost to himself: "Let's keep this in perspective, shall we? It was only four chickens."

CHAPTER 6: CRAIG

Meredith heard the low growl of Craig's motorbike approaching the garage before the dog barked a greeting from his kennel outside the front door.

She heard him shout, "Stop it, Captain!" The Collie had the annoying habit of circling people, trying to round them up, and she worried that one day there'd be an accident with a guest. A few moments later, the door slammed and Craig dropped his helmet in the hall before flinging his briefcase onto the dining table.

"How was your meeting, dear?" she asked, as though his gesture required an explanation. She'd just finished setting the table and placed a little vase of flowers from the garden in the centre.

"A complete waste of time, that's what it was," he exploded. His grey beard trembled as he shook his head.

"It feels like we're sleepwalking towards disaster on the wind turbine project. Some of us had another go at trying to find out what's happening, but the mayor just shuts down the conversation. Bloody Mathieu."

"Did you put it on the agenda?" she asked.

"Of course. But that hypocrite just says there's nothing new. Another one who was grinning was the dairy farmer who agreed to a substation on his land and who naturally kept quiet about it." He sat down at the head of the long oak table, scowling.

"Isn't that a conflict of interest?"

"He should have declared an interest, yes. But nobody made a fuss about it . . ." He pulled his wife towards him, holding her by the waist. "What's for dinner?" he asked.

"Stew," she said. Since moving to France, the couple had retreated to the comfort food of their childhood, even in summer. "I didn't know what time you'd be home."

Craig went in search of a bottle of wine.

"I've opened a bottle in the kitchen," said Meredith. "I used it in the stew. It'll do."

They helped themselves to the steaming lamb stew and baked potato in the spacious dining room which opened into a lounge with a granite fireplace at one end. The downstairs rooms in the converted farmhouse were gloomy under low wooden beams. Meredith had already switched on the lights which cast a yellow glow over the fruit bowl on the table, similar to a Dutch still life.

"I think Mathieu thinks I'm the ringleader," said Craig. "He obviously thinks that I shouldn't be getting involved because we're Brits."

"Yes, but we have the same rights as everybody else who lives here. And I must say that if we were told that a turbine was going to be installed near our house, I wouldn't want it," said Meredith. "I mean, the whooshing and scraping noise from the machine, and the shadow from the blades . . ."

"Exactly. You should have heard what Mathieu said when a couple of others raised the case of Didier. He's trying to prevent three of them being put within earshot of his house. Do you know what Mathieu told him? 'It's not like you'll have a nuclear plant next door.'"

"Oh for Christ's sake," said Meredith. "So what's to be done?"

"Didier and some other locals have set up a pressure group, and I'm joining it. I mean they've already ruined the view with that wind farm on top of the hill, but now it's getting a lot closer to home. If it carries on, the village will be encircled."

Craig took out a large handkerchief from his trouser pocket and wiped his lips. "This is delicious by the way. So tender."

Meredith pushed a napkin in his direction, and acknowledged the compliment.

"It's worthwhile for the farmers to install them, isn't it?"

"Oh yes. Big time. But what about the people who end up losing money on their property? Didier says the value of his house will be devalued by forty per cent!"

"That's a lot. Do you want some more?"

Craig nodded. "Just a bit. I wouldn't want it to go to waste." It was what he said every night before accepting a second helping.

Meredith picked up his plate and went into the kitchen, returning with a large portion of stew.

"And apart from the turbines, what else?" she asked.

"Oh, Sylvie, as usual. She knows everything, she knows where all the bodies are buried, and she wants us all to know it. She's poisonous, that woman."

"She's a professional gossip. That's why she's perfect for that job," said Meredith.

She had crossed swords herself with Mme Le Goff, who continued to call her Marie despite being told that her name was Meredith. She noticed that others in the village had followed suit, shrugging their shoulders and pursing their lips in that French way when she corrected them. It wasn't outright hostility, more like indifference. Even after so many years in Louennec they were still made to feel like outsiders.

"Do you remember, I used to think that she was the mayor's secretary, when we first got here," she said. "Only later did I realise that as the *secrétaire de la mairie*, she's actually the one in charge of all the *commune*'s secrets."

"You can say that again," he said, grinning. He mopped up his remaining gravy with a piece of bread.

"Anyway, of course she brought up the death of Adam, as though I'd have some inside information about it."

"And do you?" Meredith leaned forward to listen.

"He was gay, wasn't he?"

"Was he?"

"I'm just saying that I heard he frequented gay clubs in Rennes. But obviously I didn't mention that to Sylvie or anyone else for that matter. I mean, so what?"

"Exactly," said Meredith. "And what's more it's none of that woman's business. Apple pie?"

"Homemade?"

"Of course. With our own apples."

Craig's mood had mellowed after his second glass of red.

"Anyway, it's a damned nuisance about Adam, now that he's swimming with the fishes," he said. "We'll have to find another Mother Goose."

His wife frowned. "That's not funny, Craig. But you're right, the show must go on. Maybe you can persuade Jonathan. He managed to escape when you were handing out the roles at their place."

He smiled. "That's true. Have you got the script handy? I want to have another look at it before we have them all over to do the read-through."

Meredith gestured towards a pile of papers at the other end of the table. Craig got up in search of his cigarette packet.

"Do you mind?" It was worth a try, although he knew the answer. Meredith pointed in the direction of the door.

"You might want to consider putting some more jokes in," she said. Craig pushed his chair away and picked up the script. Then, with cigarettes in hand, he went to the front door where he knew that Captain would be waiting, thumping his tail on the ground.

He turned back to Meredith before opening the door.

"Do you know who I saw this afternoon?"

"I can't imagine." Meredith stopped clearing away the table.

"Mariam. You know, Jennifer and Jonathan's daughter. I was driving back from Carhaix and I saw her on the main road, walking in the opposite direction."

"That's odd. Shouldn't she be at school?"

"That's what I thought. She didn't see me, and I wondered about saying something to her. I wouldn't want her to come to any harm."

"She's very striking, isn't she?" said Meredith. "With a natural dignity for a girl her age. Was she with her friends?"

"No. That's what struck me. She was by herself."

CHAPTER 7: A SCHOOL MEETING

Jennifer and Jonathan slammed the doors of his old Volvo and walked across the deserted school playground.

They'd been summoned to a meeting with Mariam's headmistress without explanation. Jonathan hadn't stopped grumbling about the disruption and inconvenience on the drive to Carhaix in mid-afternoon, while Jennifer looked out of the window across the fields. It was the first time in a year they'd been invited to the school outside the regular parents' evenings. By the time they reached the school, she'd gnawed the fingernail of her left index finger down to the quick.

She was surprised that Mariam wasn't present when they were shown into the spartan office of the headmistress, Mme Ducros, a short woman with a sharp nose. She got up to shake hands. Her grip was firm and businesslike.

"Thank you for coming," she said. "Please sit down. I wanted to talk to you about Mariam."

Jennifer had to stop herself asking, "What's she done wrong?" and waited.

"We have some concerns," Mme Ducros continued. Her tone was sympathetic.

"What sort of concerns?" Jonathan asked. Jennifer didn't like the aggressive sound in his voice.

"Mariam was drying a mat in class," Mme Ducros said. Jennifer didn't understand. The head repeated slowly, "*Elle sèche les cours de maths.*" She looked across at Jonathan who seemed to have understood.

"She's skipping maths," he whispered.

"The maths teacher informed me that she has missed three classes on Tuesday afternoons," said Mme Ducros. "We will have to discipline her. Can you enlighten me as to why she hasn't been attending class?"

Neither Jennifer nor Jonathan had an explanation.

"It has also been brought to my notice that she is being bullied," the head continued. "We are wondering whether the two things may be connected."

Their daughter was being bullied and playing truant. How come neither of them knew anything about this? Jonathan and Jennifer looked at each other in stunned silence. Instinctively she placed her hand on Jonathan's knee for support.

Mme Ducros went on, "I can see you are surprised. But we wondered whether there was anything you'd noticed at home? Anything changed about her behaviour?"

Jennifer glanced at Jonathan before answering. "She's definitely become more withdrawn in the time since we moved here. She spends her free time upstairs with her brother, they're online all the time. With parental restrictions, of course."

"Like all the other kids their age," Jonathan said. He stared defensively at the head.

"Where is Mariam from?" Mme Ducros asked.

"From London," said Jennifer. It was the answer she always gave.

"I mean originally," said the head.

"From Somalia. But we adopted her when she was a baby."

"I understand," the head replied. "She hasn't mentioned the bullying then? When I asked her teachers about her it seems they have observed her being teased. She looks different from the other pupils, you see."

"She doesn't seem to have made friends at school. I've asked her about that because she never brings anyone home," said Jennifer. "But I presumed that all girls of her age are hooked on social media, so that's where she'd be communicating with her friends."

She looked across at Jonathan who seemed angry. She was keenly aware that the head must be taking a dim view of their parenting. Mariam was skipping classes and they were blissfully ignorant.

Mme Ducros cleared her throat. "We have a counsellor here at the school who may be able to help Mariam. But I wanted to see you first to find out how much you knew about this situation," she went on. "It's important that you give her an opportunity to talk to you about her feelings. Please keep in touch."

"Thank you," said Jennifer. She could tell that Jonathan couldn't wait to get out.

As soon as they were out of the building, Jonathan exploded. "This is so embarrassing, being called in to see the head," he said. "Skipping classes! Mariam will never get anywhere unless she knuckles down."

"Embarrassing for whom? For us? What about poor Mariam! What if we're to blame? We're so busy trying to make ends meet that we had no idea that she had problems at school."

"Well, you'd better talk to her," he said, opening the car doors. "I've got work to do. The Dow is down on the jobs report. And you've got the school run in a bit."

"Look," she responded. "She's our daughter and we have to present a united front. Maybe Luke had picked up hints about what was going on. No wonder she's so withdrawn if she's being bullied. It's awful."

They sat in silence for a while as Jonathan drove. Then Jennifer said, "What about the parental controls, anyway? I always felt the kids were safe upstairs on their computers. I mean, Madame Ducros didn't say whether it was online bullying, did she?"

"She's got the phone too. Kids are much more savvy than we are online, let's face it."

"But what do you want to do? Take her phone off her? That wouldn't solve anything! If she's playing truant, we need to know where the hell she's going."

They reached the village. "That's where Pippa lives," Jennifer said, pointing to a cul-de-sac on their left.

Jonathan braked sharply, jerking her head back against the headrest. He hadn't noticed the hearse parked outside the church on the main street just along from the cul-de-sac. Jennifer craned her neck to look at a small group of mourners going inside.

"Oh for goodness' sake, be careful!" she said. "It must be Adam's funeral. I'd completely forgotten about it because of having to go to Mariam's school."

"But he wasn't a particular friend of ours, was he, apart from him finding our house? Anyway, we've both got too much work on," said Jonathan. "I've got to get back right now."

He accelerated again, ignoring the 30 kph sign ahead of a speed bump which caused the car to land with a bounce.

"We should have gone. I mean he did die in our garden a month ago," she said.

Jonathan slowed down the car and looked at her. He still seemed to be irritated after their meeting with the school head.

"Do you want to go? It's not too late. I can drop you here and you can walk back to the church," he said.

Jennifer checked the time on her phone.

"Oh never mind," she said. "I feel bad but you're right, we don't really have the time. And I'll have to go back to pick up the kids anyway."

They passed cows with straining udders grazing in a field and the rounded huts of the pig farm before turning off down a lane framed by oak trees that led to their smallholding. Jonathan pulled into the drive, got out of the car and went inside without a word.

CHAPTER 8: MARIAM

Luke waved goodbye to two of his schoolfriends in the yard and had to be practically dragged to the car so they could get back to Mariam's school in Carhaix on time.

Jennifer caught sight of Emma at the village school gate talking to another parent as she pulled out of her parking space with Luke beside her. She must be waiting for Romy, who was in Luke's class.

Luke got out a bag of Haribos and chattered away beside her. How could two children be so different? she wondered. They'd both had exactly the same upbringing in London, but what had happened to Mariam? Were people so racist here that they'd destroyed her daughter's confidence? Or was it something deeper, a long buried trauma to do with her short life in Somalia and Kenya that was resurfacing now that she'd reached puberty? Or maybe it was simply that time of life and they had all better brace themselves for her teenage years.

She felt Luke prodding her arm. He wanted to know if they could go to the fairground in Carhaix at the weekend.

"I've got the market on Saturday morning," she said. "Maybe Daddy can take you."

He didn't seem convinced by this. Neither was she. Lately Jonathan had taken to doing errands or playing golf on the weekend as soon as she got in.

Mariam was waiting for them outside the school gate. She was standing a distance away from a group of pupils who were drifting off after class. Jennifer supposed that most of them lived in town. Mariam was bent over her phone and only looked up when Jennifer sounded the horn. She got into the back without a greeting. *Just like her father.*

"Everything OK?" Jennifer asked, hoping her voice sounded as natural as possible. She was still weighing whether to mention the meeting with the headmistress. Probably better to wait until they got home, she thought.

Byron came to meet them, his tail wagging, as the car approached the house, its downstairs windows framed by granite surrounds. Mariam looked as though she was going straight upstairs, but Jennifer stopped her.

"I need a word with you," she said in a low voice. Luke, oblivious to what was going on, petted the dog and went off to count the hens. He'd done so meticulously ever since the weasel attack. He said he was "on patrol", with all the seriousness of an eight-year-old.

Jennifer set Mariam down on the sofa and sat next to her. She spoke gently, fearing that she would flounce off.

"Your father and I are worried about you."

Mariam shifted in her seat.

"You know that we're here for you if you want to talk . . ." Jennifer began. She reached out to touch Mariam's arm, but her daughter pulled back sharply.

"I can understand it's been a difficult time for you, what with the move and a new school and everything. You can tell me . . ."

They sat staring at each other for a moment, brown eyes on green, unblinking.

"We heard they've been teasing you at school. Tell me what's going on . . ."

Mariam seemed unsure whether to respond. Eventually she said, "They call me names."

"What sort of names?"

"*Mariam musulmane*. That's what they chant. Am I Muslim?"

Jennifer leaned towards her and folded her into a long embrace. Was this the moment to tell her? She'd often wondered when this awkward moment would come, when she'd have to admit that they knew nothing of her parentage. Mariam didn't even have a birth certificate. All they knew was that because she was Somali she was most likely to have come from a Muslim background. Had they been wrong to erase her heritage? Who could help her answer this question? These thoughts swirled around in Jennifer's head. Mariam had begun to sob, her slim body convulsed.

"I don't belong here!" she said. *None of us do*, thought Jennifer. "I hate myself," Mariam went on, still crying. She leaned back as the sobs subsided and wiped her eyes on the sleeve of her hoodie.

"I'm so sorry," Jennifer repeated, her own voice trembling. "We love you."

She heard footsteps on the stairs and looked round to see Jonathan.

"What's going on here?" he said.

Mariam pulled away from Jennifer and said, "Nothing." Her face was contorted by tears.

"So what's all this we hear about you skipping maths classes?" he said. Jennifer flashed an angry look in his direction and reached out towards Mariam who stood up.

"What's it to you?" Mariam responded with unexpected violence. Jonathan opened his mouth to reply but before he could do so she'd headed for the stairs. He turned to follow her before thinking better of it.

"Thanks a lot for your support," Jennifer said, her voice laden with sarcasm.

"I only came down because I could hear it wasn't going so well for you."

"We're going to have to be very careful about how we proceed here. She says she doesn't belong here, and that she hates herself. So, whatever is going on it's deep. And frankly, I don't think that either you or I are equipped to deal with it."

"You're dead right there," he said. "What about the headmistress? Didn't she say they could help with problem children?"

"First of all, I wouldn't call her a problem child," said Jennifer. "And it's obvious that skipping maths is just the tip of the iceberg. We need to find out just who exactly is bullying her. I could kill them. And their parents."

Jonathan made a sound that sounded like a cross between a cough and a grunt.

"We'll talk about this later," he said. Then he muttered something about the markets and left Jennifer with her head buried in a sofa cushion.

CHAPTER 9: A DEMONSTRATION

A crowd had gathered outside the *mairie* that same evening when Pippa came home from her class in Rennes.

Before she turned into her street, she saw Craig addressing about twenty people, waving his arms around. She parked the car in the drive, and went back to see him bellowing from on top of a plastic crate.

"*C'est du bullshit!*" he yelled. "We had a vote on the council which rejected the installation of wind turbines in Louennec. The vote — wait for it — was three in favour and eleven against! And I know because I'm on the council!"

There was a ripple of applause before he went on: "But what happened? We were ignored! The mayor sent off the planning application to the prefect!"

"So, what do we do now?" someone called out from the crowd which had spilled onto the street. Pippa caught sight of Derek, clad in lycra gear with shorts on top, jogging towards them. He was as surprised to see them as they were him, and the crowd parted to let him past. He waved to Craig on his way through.

"Join our association," Craig continued. "We're going to challenge it all the way to court, that's what we're going to do! Starting with a petition!" His accented French didn't seem to deter any of his audience, his passion was carrying the day. He beckoned to a young man and said: "Didier, tell them about your house."

Didier stood on the crate and shouted, "The only people in France who benefit from turbines are the developers! They want to build three on land next to my house which will drive down its value, and drive my family mad from the noise. They want to pour tons of concrete into the ground which will kill off biodiversity. Look over there" — he pointed towards the hills — "they are monsters. You can see their red lights blinking at night. Who will visit our beautiful region anymore? And the council is in the developers' pockets!" This drew rousing boos from the crowd. Pippa studied the faces but didn't recognise anyone apart from Craig.

A small group stood apart from the demonstrators, outside the café. Out of the corner of one eye, she noticed Yann watching the proceedings attentively.

"Not only that, but they're trying to split the villagers apart. The mayor stands back and does nothing as one by one, the farmers in Louennec are being paid for accepting these eyesores. What do we say?" Didier shouted.

"No!" came the reply. Some of the protesters held up placards. Nobody else went to the front to speak and the gathering dispersed. Some headed for the café. Yann had disappeared.

Craig spotted Pippa and joined her.

"Wow, you got them all fired up there," she said.

"It's about time. I'm fed up with Mathieu, the mayor. I might have to stand down for a while to fight our corner on this, or he'll tell me it's a conflict of interest. But honestly it makes no economic or ecological sense to go ahead."

"I'm with you on that," said Pippa. "Those turbines on the hilltop over there are an awful eyesore. And anyway don't wind farms only contribute a small amount to the electricity grid in France?"

"Absolutely. Onshore wind only provides a small percentage. But they're now developing offshore, big time, which should take the pressure off communities like ours.

Not to mention nuclear, of course. But it's the hypocrisy that gets me."

"You're probably not the most popular person on the council then," she said with a smile.

"Exactly . . . and frankly, no matter how many years you've lived here, you'll always be one of *les Anglais*, as you'll find out. After all this time, Meredith and I don't really feel like we've been accepted by the villagers."

Pippa thought back to her meeting with Mme Le Goff at the *mairie*, who had stressed all the obstacles she faced in order to open her bakery.

"That's a shame."

"Look at the council vote though," Craig continued. "The majority agree with me, but they're not vocal enough. Two of them who voted to approve the wind turbines here were both farmers who stand to gain if they agree to let them be installed on their land. And Mathieu was the third."

"But do you really think you can stop it when it's national policy and with so many financial interests involved?" Pippa asked.

"Honestly? I doubt it. But at least we should be able to delay the procedure, maybe for a decade. Who knows? I may be dead by then anyway!"

CHAPTER 10: A DUNKING

"I'm off, then," Craig called out to Meredith from the hall. "I'm taking Captain."

"Yes, dear," he heard her say. The Collie jumped up as soon as the door opened.

"Come on," Craig commanded. He went over to his Triumph which he'd left outside the house and carefully walked it along the footpath to the garage, where he wheeled the bike in and shut the door. He looked up at the scudding clouds. The Breton summer was too short to envisage many motorbike outings, and he was lucky to still enjoy his rides in mid-October.

He set off along the track in a light breeze. Craig enjoyed his daily constitutional. Sometimes he would go down to the stream which led to the river. Or he might go into the woods behind the house and through the fields. But his favourite walk took him on a circular route above the village. He knew that the locals laughed at him behind his back. None of them went walking for pleasure, for them the countryside was their workplace.

The dog ran on ahead, looking back from time to time to check that he was following. The circuit took him up a lane past the dairy farm, where at this time of the afternoon the cows were being herded into the milk shed. Then he'd take a track which had sweeping views over the valley and beyond, to the ridge where the row of hated wind turbines marred the view.

He'd often listen to a podcast, or a Radio 4 programme, as he strolled along. But today, his mind was on the Christmas pantomime. He'd hoped that Adam would have put out the word to his clients, as for the first time they were holding the panto in the village hall and therefore had a bigger space to fill. Now he'd have to ask Derek for help in drumming up an audience from among his British clients in the surrounding villages grouped into the *commune*. Maybe Jennifer and Pippa could mention it to their market customers. They weren't expecting many French to show up for the performance. He took a deep breath of fresh air, then stooped to pick up a small branch lying at the foot of a hedge. This would serve as his walking stick.

After about fifteen minutes they began climbing the lane that led to the farm. Captain had his nose to the wind and Craig dawdled behind, lost in his thoughts. Looking ahead, he could see the cattle crowding together as they crossed the lane in the distance. He saw a figure among them, and recognised him as Didier, the farm hand. Then he saw two other people among the cows. He stopped for a moment to watch them. What were those two guys doing? Didier didn't need any help to guide the cows to the milking shed. As he watched, he realised there seemed to be some sort of struggle going on among the three of them.

"Captain!" he shouted, and pointed ahead. The dog broke into a run and Craig followed at his own pace. As he got closer, he couldn't believe his eyes. Didier was being manhandled over a concrete wall into the slurry tank.

"*Arrêtez!*" he cried out, brandishing his stick, but his voice rebounded in the breeze. Captain was closing in and his bark had attracted the attackers' attention. Craig heard a loud splash as the victim fell into the slurry and his two assailants ran off. Captain had reached the scene, but instead of chasing after the men, he was distracted by the cows. By the time Craig reached the farmyard there was chaos, the mooing beasts running in all directions, their udders swaying.

He was panting heavily. He took one look at the pit and realised that there was no hope of him dragging out Didier, who was lying face down, motionless, in the stinking morass. With Captain following behind him, he turned reluctantly towards the farmhouse to seek help. The farmer was one of the council members who supported the wind farm project.

The man's wife opened the door. *"Ça va, Monsieur?"*

She seemed concerned that he was out of breath, and he was so agitated that his words came out in a mixture of French and English. But he saw her concern turn to alarm as he described the drowning. By this time her husband had joined her, frowning as soon as he recognised Craig.

Craig pointed with his stick towards the slurry tank and hastened back in that direction, with Captain hot on his heels. The farmer disappeared inside and re-emerged a few moments later wearing a pullover and carrying his phone.

When he caught up with Craig he said, "I've called the *gendarmerie*."

* * *

Meredith heard a commotion outside and opened the front door just as two gendarmes were driving off after dropping off Craig at the house.

She switched on the porch light and saw Craig pointing to the kennel in the garden. Captain slunk off with a sideways glance at her, his head bowed. Craig then grasped her tightly, as though struggling to stay on his feet. His face was damp with tears. She hadn't seen him like this since he lost his job on a London paper, years earlier.

"It's Didier," he said.

"Didier?"

"You remember . . . the young guy from the village who lent us the rope when we did Jack and the Beanstalk last

Christmas? In fact, I was going to ask him to help us out again this year."

"Ah yes, Didier. Such a nice young man. Do you remember the children climbing up it?"

Craig didn't reply. He obviously wasn't in the mood for jollity.

"Come in, dear, tell me everything," said Meredith, leading him inside.

They sat down at the dining room table where Craig took his usual position at the head of the table, with Meredith beside him. She squeezed his hand as she listened.

"How awful! Who would do such a thing!" she asked, once he'd told her everything he'd seen.

Craig shook his head.

"It must have been planned in advance. They'd know exactly when he'd be taking the cows in for milking. And they'd need two of them to heave him in. I'd never have been strong enough to save him."

Meredith wrinkled her nose at the thought. "And what about Captain?"

"Frankly, he was a damned nuisance. He came with us to town, and they left him in a car while I went in to the *gendarmerie*. But they kept me waiting to give my statement so that's why it took so long for me to get home."

"Didn't you say it was Didier who's in charge of the anti-wind turbine association?"

Craig glowered. "My God, you're right. Of course, why didn't I think of that! He must have been killed because he was trying to stop the wind farm development in Louennec. I should have mentioned that to the gendarmes.

"He also has a nice young wife and a daughter," he went on. "I don't know how they're going to cope. I mean he didn't earn much from being a farm hand, and I think she only works part-time. I'll go and see her tomorrow."

"I think I remember him saying that he made that rope he lent us," said Meredith.

"Oh yes, he grows hemp," said Craig. "He inherited a field over the other side of the village and his grandfather had a rope-making machine. But they're not going to get rich on that, are they?"

He got up and wandered into the kitchen, where he opened the fridge.

"What's for dinner?" he asked.

"Confit de canard," she called out. "And mashed potato. It won't take long."

He took out two beers and brought them back to the table.

"I say, dear," said Meredith. "You don't think there's any connection between Didier's and Adam's deaths, do you?"

CHAPTER 11: THE PLAY'S THE THING

The Louennec players trouped into Craig and Meredith's dining room where drinks and nibbles had been set out.

Meredith invited the guests to help themselves to the food and wine from the table before taking their places in the sitting room. "There's red and white, and fizzy water. I can make coffee later for those who want some."

They sat on folding plastic chairs around the fireplace, placing glasses on the floor and balancing plates on their knees. Craig handed out a script to everyone.

"Here's yours, Jonathan. I've taken the executive decision to give you the starring role of Mother Goose because of Adam's untimely death."

Everyone applauded but Jonathan looked dismayed. Emma, who was sitting next to him, dug him in the ribs. "Go on," she said. "It'll be fun. I'm playing Billy Gosling, your son!"

But he didn't seem persuaded.

"Look, it has to be a man, and it was between you and Mark, as we need Derek to play the songs," said Craig, impatiently. "I think Mark will be relieved not to be picked, isn't that true?"

His remark caught Mark by surprise just as he was emptying a bottle of red wine into his glass. But he nodded his head vigorously. Jonathan was now resigned to his fate.

"By the way," said Craig. "You'll have heard about the horrible death in the village, which I'm sorry to say I actually witnessed two days ago. But has anyone heard anything about Adam? I saw in the paper that it wasn't drugs that killed him, and that they're investigating a suspicious drowning. But nobody had any more information at the funeral the other day. We were wondering whether the two deaths might be connected."

"Really?" said Jennifer. "I had to take a picture of the dairy farmer for the paper yesterday. What a terrible thing to happen! We've certainly not heard anything else about the investigation into Adam's death."

"The gendarme who lives next to me said they hoped to get data from his phone that might be helpful," said Pippa. "It's so sad about Didier being killed. I'd seen him at an anti-wind farm demonstration with Craig only a few days ago and I did wonder if it's got anything to do with his activities."

"*Cui bono*, my dear Pippa," thundered Craig. "If you ask me, the finger of suspicion points directly towards the developers of the wind farm project, although I'd never have thought they'd go that far. I was out with Captain when I saw poor Didier being pitched into the slurry tank of the dairy farm where he worked. But I was too far away to identify the two men who pushed him."

"Isn't Didier the one who lent us the rope for last year's panto? Jack and the Beanstalk?" asked Derek.

"It was indeed," came the reply.

"Oh dear. Tragic," said Derek, shaking his head. "He was very helpful. That's how I found out that the Bretons have been growing hemp for centuries."

"What a mine of information you are, Derek," said Craig. Nobody knew if he was being sarcastic.

Meredith touched Craig's arm to suggest it was time to start the run-through. Craig picked up his script and proclaimed, "Act one, Scene one. Mother Goose is sitting outside her house with Billy Gosling. Priscilla enters."

Pippa looked up. "Craig, do you need to read the stage instructions? I mean we can all see what's written down."

"In my experience as director, it helps to situate the action. But if you wish . . ." he said. "Yes," they all chimed in.

"All right. Now. Please go ahead, Mother Goose," he said, looking at Jonathan.

"Hello, my dear," he said in a high-pitched squawk. "Look who's here! I wasn't *eggs-pecting* you."

Pippa raised a hand. "Excuse me, but is he supposed to be talking in a woman's voice? I thought the pantomime dames keep their own male voice. That's part of the fun, isn't it?"

Craig made a clicking noise with his tongue. "Sorry, but can we crack on? We'll never get through it if we keep stopping all the time. I'm fine with Jonathan's voice however he wants to do it. We can discuss it later. Now Pippa . . ."

She made a loud quacking noise which met with Craig's approval.

Emma was next to speak in the role of Billy, fluttering her eyelashes at Mother Goose who smiled back. Then it was Jennifer's turn, as the squire's daughter.

"Isn't this a role for one of the children?" she asked after reading out her first line. "I mean, she's obviously supposed to be a child, and I'm thirty-six!"

"Jennifer my dear, this is *pantomime*," said Craig. "We'll get you a wig with pigtails, that's all you need."

Reluctantly, she ploughed on. Mark, playing the squire, read his lines in a monotone, and was stopped by the director.

"Come on, Mark," he said. "You can do better than that! This is a great role!" All eyes were on Mark. How would he react to this criticism? He glared at Craig before taking a long swig of wine. Then he carried on regardless, lecturing Mother Goose about what would happen to her if she didn't pay the rent.

Meredith waved her arms around when her turn came as Fairy Nuff.

"Can Solenn get me a magic wand?" she asked. Everyone's eyes searched the room for Solenn who was sitting next to Derek, reading something on her phone.

Then Craig proceeded to keep on interrupting Meredith's performance, commenting from time to time, "We'll need a joke in here."

The evening wore on and the alcohol flowed. They all cried out "Oh no he isn't!" and "Oh yes he is!" at the appropriate points without prompting from Craig who seemed well pleased with the result. He hammed it up as the Demon King, causing the others to boo and hiss from the sidelines. Mark didn't seem to be paying any attention to the script after saying his own lines: he had one of Meredith's homemade sausage rolls in one hand, and a refill of red wine in the other.

It was 9.30 p.m. when they finished the read-through.

"Derek will compose a rousing finale for us, something about loving one's neighbours, won't you?" said Craig. He beamed at the group. "Anyone want one for the road?"

"Not me, thanks," said Jonathan. "I'm driving." The others also demurred.

They stood around while jackets and bags were collected. Meredith handed Jennifer her jacket, saying in a low voice, "Is everything all right?"

Jennifer frowned. "I'm sorry. What do you mean?"

"I mean with your daughter, my dear," Meredith replied. "It's just that Craig mentioned that he'd seen her one afternoon when she should have been at school."

"Oh that, yes," said Jennifer with a forced smile. "Don't worry, we're on it. She's just been having a bit of trouble at school." She turned away and asked nobody in particular, "Does anyone need a lift?"

Pippa and Emma both had their own cars. Mark was also intending to drive home, although he seemed a little unsteady.

"Are you sure you're OK to drive?" Jonathan asked. None of them knew Mark very well despite most of them taking advantage of his accountant's background for their tax declarations. Jennifer imagined that if it weren't for the annual pantomime, his social life would consist of propping up the bar at the café in Louennec before staggering home to watch Netflix.

"Yes, no worries," said Mark, unconvincingly.

Captain appeared from nowhere as soon as Craig opened the front door, and began sniffing round their ankles. Mark made as though to give him a kick to get him out of the way.

"I was thinking about props, but we can see later," said Craig, before waving them off. "Meredith will have a word with Solenn about that as she'll be doing the costumes. And finding a wig for Jennifer. Has anyone got a gun, by the way?"

CHAPTER 12: BARE BOTTOMS

Jennifer was up to her elbows in feathers in her "lab" when she heard the car door slam.

"Can you give me a hand?" she called out to Jonathan.

She always had to ask him if he could help out with preparing the chickens for market. They were the Naked Neck breed, and looked strange when they foraged in the chicken run with the other hens. They'd never let them roam free because of the dog, even though he'd struggle to catch one. Jennifer was sometimes aware that her customers laughed at her mispronunciation of *cous nus* in French. She couldn't help saying *culs nus* which she now knew meant bare bottoms.

She was halfway through her afternoon's work. It took a couple of hours to prepare the broilers for market each month, including scooping out the giblets. She could never have imagined, when they were discussing their move in Hackney, that she'd be making money from killing poultry in France. She'd never killed anything until then, not even a spider, as far as she could remember. But now here she was, raising chicks destined for slaughter so that every three to four weeks she would be back in her personal abattoir.

Jonathan joined her and the two of them worked in silence, finishing the job. Soon, the fifteen chickens were laid out neatly side by side in the shed. Some she'd deliver to private customers, leaving ten for the market.

"Thanks," she said. "By the way, I spoke to the headmistress about what Mariam told me."

"What do you mean?"

"I mean what she said about her classmates calling her *Mariam, musulmane*. That's obviously the bullying Madame Ducros was talking about. I told her how upsetting it is for us and that she had to put a stop to it. But she wouldn't give me the name of the child, or the children, who are doing it. I mean it's racist, or sectarian, whatever you want to call it."

"Good grief, Jennifer! You didn't go there, did you? She's a *child*. Do you think she's going to start wearing the hijab or something? As far as I'm concerned, she's our daughter, and she's been raised in England by our family since she was a baby and that's it! We adopted her from one of the poorest countries in the world and surely it's irrelevant whether she's Muslim or Catholic or Buddhist. I mean WTF, Jen?"

"Yes. I know. But remember that we discussed this with the adoption agency when we came back with her. About being sensitive to her heritage. I mean what if we've deprived her of her identity?"

He put the knife he was holding on to the counter, shaking his head.

"Look. This is the first time this has ever come up. Back home there were Somali kids in her school, but none of them were her friends, were they? And there's no chance we could ever travel to her country or even find her birth mother because of the circumstances that we both know about . . ." He paused. "Anyway what did Madame Ducros say?"

"She said she'd punish the offenders. And that Mariam had already seen the counsellor."

"Good. So we've finished here, right?" He looked around the small tiled shed.

"Yes."

He turned to go, but she could tell he was still brooding.

"Anyway we're in the right place if she's being bullied because of her heritage," he remarked, turning back.

"What do you mean?" Jennifer realised he was probably referring to France's strict secularism.

"Never mind." He shook his head. "I'm going to pick some tomatoes. Look, children aren't racist, are they? They're colour blind. It's the parents who are racist."

He was probably right about that, she thought. She began clearing up the mess on the counter before realising he was still standing motionless behind her. "Did you see Emma today?" she asked over her shoulder.

"I did actually. In fact I see her most days when I pick up Luke."

"Oh yes, sorry." There had to be an innocent explanation. Jennifer wondered why she was apologising. Then she cast her mind back to the read-through when she'd noticed Jonathan staring admiringly at Emma as she read her lines, openly flirting with him. And she remembered when, a month earlier at their party in the garden, they'd disappeared into the living room for their private conversation.

She turned back to the counter, still not feeling reassured, and heard Jonathan walk out of the shed.

* * *

The next day, Jennifer and Pippa had agreed to meet after the Saturday market. Jennifer surveyed the scene from her stall before packing up at 12.30. It was a cold late October morning, and everyone wore an extra layer of clothes. Groups of villagers were exchanging gossip in front of the charcuterie wagon where there was always a long queue. By now she knew most of the stallholders by sight, including the cheesemonger, the fishmonger, and the crêpe seller, not to mention the charcutier and other organic producers like herself. But she never chatted to the people selling clothes and accessories. Derek's wife Solenn seemed to be the only one selling genuine Breton items on her jewellery stall, although she wasn't there that morning. The rest was just cheap tat from China. She glanced across at Pippa who was talking to a couple of customers, and was glad that things seemed to be looking up for her.

Pippa was waiting for her on a leatherette bench when Jennifer arrived in the warmth of the Central Café.

They took off their coats, hats and scarves. "God, it's so cold out there. And I've got two other layers on under this polo neck," Pippa complained. They ordered drinks from the waiter who mentioned that rain was on the way, which he seemed to think would be an improvement.

"You were busy today," Jennifer said.

"I decided to mix it up a bit. I thought that I might as well do some baking, and all the cup cakes and rum babas went in minutes. I wish I could say the same for the curry," said Pippa, ruefully. "But I live in hope."

"It must be good practice for your course, the baking?"

"Well, the course is basically baguettes, pain de campagne and pastries. And we cook in these huge industrial-sized ovens. So, at home I practise some things like croissants, or the brioches like the rum babas, but also cakes. I thought it would be interesting to see what sells before I open the shop. What about you, how was your market day?"

Jennifer finished her small café noisette in two sips. It was strong and bitter. She watched Pippa cradle her hot chocolate and wished she'd chosen the same. "Oh, we're busy too. I sold all my homemade jams today. And at this time of year we're spending all our spare time picking fruit and vegetables for freezing. Sometimes it's hard to find the time when I get called out on a job for the paper."

"At least you get to meet the locals that way."

"Yes, but the people I see for work are mostly farmers round here. We've not got much in common really. I mean taking a picture of a prize bull isn't exactly a bonding experience." She smiled. "Although it can be when it deposits steaming dung all over your shoes."

"Oh no!"

"Back home, we were friendly with other schoolchildren's parents. That's not happened here so far. But it's early days . . . by the way, I had a look at your crowdfunding page. It looks great. I liked the way you broke down the 10,000 euros, one part for the renovation and the other to go towards the equipment."

"Thank you," said Pippa. "I thought it was best to explain it in French, as the villagers will be my main customers. Mind you, the actual costs are going to be much higher. My main expense is going to be paying a sidekick as I won't be able to run the shop on my own. As a so-called company boss I have to pay a huge percentage on top of my employee's salary in social contributions."

"Yes I know. I guess that's the price of the French welfare system. It's also why I never took anyone on to help out on the smallholding. I prefer to manage by myself. But I'm sure you'll reach your target."

Pippa grimaced. "I hope so. Did you notice I mentioned on the site that I'll be selling sausage rolls? I thought that might pique the villagers' curiosity."

Jennifer laughed. "I did. We'll be round!"

She was beginning to gather her things together when Pippa asked, "How's your daughter doing?"

She didn't answer immediately, wondering whether to confide in Pippa. But who else was there?

"Actually, not great. She's been bullied, teased about being Muslim. But also she's playing truant. I need to get to the bottom of it. But it's obviously thrown up all sorts of stuff about her feeling that she doesn't belong."

"I'm so sorry, Jennifer. That's tough," she said. "Talking of adopted children, I saw a fascinating interview on television the other night with the creative director of Balmain. I can't remember his name but he was explaining that he was adopted and became obsessed with finding his birth mother."

"And did he find her?"

"He managed to find her address in France and wrote her a letter which he never posted. It was very moving, because he said that he was worried that she might reject him a second time, having abandoned him when he was a baby. I think he hoped that his real mum might see the interview and get in touch. He made a documentary about the whole thing."

Jennifer listened intently. There was no chance they could ever put Mariam in touch with her birth family.

Pippa went on, "Anyway the Balmain guy said that he loved his adoptive parents, and grandparents, who are white. But he talked about growing up and realising he was different."

"Oh really? That's so much like Mariam." Jennifer sighed. "I only hope we all get through this period unscathed. I think that now she's nearly a teenager there are things that we never thought about when she was small. We were just so happy about finding a baby to love."

Pippa squeezed Jennifer's hand.

"I'm sure she'll be fine," she said.

"When's the next panto rehearsal by the way?" she added after a pause.

"It will be in a couple of weeks at Derek and Solenn's house. It's their turn," said Jennifer. "They've got a beautiful place down by the river."

"I'm so glad I've got no lines to learn, I just need to know when to say quack quack!"

"You've got the best part, apart from Craig as the Demon King," said Jennifer.

"Jonathan doesn't seem too pleased to be Mother Goose," Pippa commented. Jennifer gave a wry smile.

"I don't think he likes making a fool of himself, not like the rest of us," she said.

"Mark is Mister Zero Charisma, isn't he?" Pippa continued. "It's as though he can't be bothered to make the effort. I wonder why he even shows up, frankly. It's probably just for the booze."

"He certainly doesn't seem to care very much for Craig," said Jennifer. "Nor his dog. But then Jonathan doesn't like Captain either. He's scared of being tripped up."

"I'm not a big fan of Craig either. He obviously feels he can throw his considerable weight around because he's on the council."

"I don't know why he insisted on my playing Mark's daughter. I don't think a wig with pigtails is going to make any difference," said Jennifer.

"I don't think it will matter to the audience. I mean most of the people there will have seen a panto before."

"But probably won't want to again!"

CHAPTER 13: A CONVERSATION

The next evening, after dinner, Jennifer decided to take the bull by the horns.

She left Jonathan doing the washing-up and knocked on Mariam's bedroom door. Inside, she found her sitting at her desk by the window overlooking the front garden and the rolling fields beyond.

"Are you doing your homework?" she asked.

Mariam nodded, and lowered her head over a notebook as if she didn't wish to be disturbed.

"Come and sit here with me," Jennifer said, patting the bed. Mariam had brought her childhood dolls with her from London. They were propped up on the pillows, staring at them with dark-brown eyes.

Mariam sighed, took off her glasses, closed her notebook and plopped herself next to Jennifer.

"We want you to be happy here," said Jennifer. "So, I want you to tell me honestly how things are going at school. What did the school counsellor say?"

"She said she knew that I'd been bullied and said she'd make sure it stopped. She asked me where I came from and I said London."

"Good for you," said Jennifer. "Did you tell her you're adopted?"

She nodded. "And then she asked me where I came from originally. So I told her. She says I'm the only pupil they've ever had from Somalia."

"Really? How special," said Jennifer. She put her arm round Mariam who didn't resist. "You must tell me who's been bullying you," she added, gently. Mariam shook her head.

"Well, at least tell me if it's girls or boys." She squeezed her shoulder.

Mariam seemed to be considering a response. Eventually, she said, "It's a girl." Raising her voice, she added, "But I'm not telling you who it is."

Jennifer frowned. *The girls were even worse than the boys.*

"All right," she said. "But at least can you tell me where you've been going to instead of attending maths lessons?"

Again, her daughter didn't reply straight away. "I go for walks," she said eventually.

"You mean you walk around Carhaix on your own?"

"Yes, of course."

Jennifer said gently, "Look, Mariam, we're worried about you. If you're out on your own instead of at school, you might get into trouble. Please, please stop this."

She realised that Mariam was shutting down. She tried another tack.

"Do you remember you asked me about whether you're Muslim? Honestly, even now, I don't know how to answer you. Religion is complicated. I mean Daddy and I aren't religious, we were both brought up as Christians in the Anglican Church. But what does that mean to us today? Probably weddings and Christmas carols, and that's it," she said.

Mariam smiled.

"That's why we never talk about religion at home. Now, if you'd grown up in France, you might be Catholic. If you'd grown up in Somalia, it's very likely you would have been raised in the Islamic faith. And if you'd been somewhere else in Africa, you might have ended up in the Christian religion, or following Islam, or something else like believing in spirits. So now that you're getting older, it will be up to you. You can read about it, you can get advice, if you're interested. Maybe you'll end up deciding that none of it is for you, like we did. But what those kids said to you was hateful. They said that because you're different, that's all. But remember that different doesn't mean bad. That's why I say you're special. Do you understand me, Mariam?"

She hadn't expected to deliver a speech, but she could see that she was getting through. Mariam's head was bowed. Jennifer stroked her hair.

"Now I'll leave you to your homework. And don't forget to ask Daddy if you need help with your maths."

CHAPTER 14: A VIEW FROM THE HILL

Pippa had found a quiet spot above the village from where she had a commanding view over the valley.

The church spire and the cluster of cream-coloured houses on the main street were just below her. The autumn foliage was a riot of colour. She unfolded her easel and examined her box of watercolours. The air was still, and puffy white clouds hung motionless in the sky.

She studied the bell tower. How delicate it was, eroded by pollution over the centuries, high above the slate roof of the church. She began sketching, placing the church on the left of her composition and imagining branches of autumn leaves through which the spire would be revealed. Looking across the valley, the row of wind turbines rose above the trees on the summit of the hill. She sighed. That blot on the landscape wouldn't be in her picture.

By mid-afternoon she'd been standing still for so long that her legs had gone stiff. She put down her paintbrush and stretched her arms above her head. The painting, with its splashes of red and orange, was coming along nicely. When she heard a popping sound across the valley, she glanced down and saw two men, holding rifles and accompanied by dogs, walking slowly across an open field. She watched them for a while but lost interest after they disappeared into a copse in the distance. She was then thinking about going home when she heard the sound of a car pulling up outside the café-tabac below her in the village. The locals would drop into the café, just along from her future bakery on the main street, for all sorts of essentials as well as tobacco, or just for a drink and a chat. But she'd never yet set foot inside.

Craning her neck to see, she recognised Jonathan's Volvo. He got out and went inside. He came out a few moments later with a packet of cigarettes. Strange. She didn't think that either of them smoked... Then she noticed someone was in the passenger seat. It was Emma. The car then continued on its way in the direction of Carhaix.

"Bastard," she said out loud. Just when that kid needs her father the most, he's got his mind on something, or someone, else.

Her first instinct was to take out her phone and tell Jennifer. But what business was it of hers? Couples had secrets, she thought. What if Jennifer was already aware of the situation? Or maybe there was a risk that her phone call to Jennifer might be responsible for the break-up of a marriage and a family.

She picked up her things and made her way slowly down a path to the main street. Her shop was boarded up, awaiting deliveries and the availability of local workmen. But the sight was a source of pride, a concrete symbol of what success could mean. She couldn't wait to start her apprenticeship on the next stage of her journey.

But her thoughts were interrupted by a blood-curdling scream from a detached house on the corner across the street, surrounded by a wooden fence. It was a woman's voice, followed by at least one man shouting. She'd heard about the elderly woman who'd ended up sharing her home with her two stepsons after her husband's death, and presumed this was her. Now she could hear loud swearing. What were the men doing home in the middle of the afternoon? She looked at the house where the shutters were closed. Should she go across to ask whether the woman was all right?

The house door was opened and slammed loudly. A male voice said something like, "If you do anything like that again I'll break your leg!" She heard someone get into a car which then came into view, emerging from the side street and accelerating as he turned the corner towards Pippa. The middle-aged driver, his hair unkempt and face flushed, glared at her. She wondered whether she should check on the woman. She was a neighbour after all. But what if the other guy opened the door?

She passed the *mairie* where a couple of anti-turbine protesters had left their banners propped against the wall. They read: "*Non aux éoliens à Louennec!*" She recognised Mme Le Goff, who greeted her coolly. Pippa presumed she was on her way home as she was holding her car keys.

"Ah Madame, how are you? I see the wind turbines aren't popular here," she said, pointing to the banners.

The Frenchwoman, her blonde hair scraped back into a bun, shrugged her shoulders. Her heavy make-up, eyebrows plucked into a curve of permanent surprise, only reinforced her forbidding appearance.

"Oh that," she said, dismissively. "It won't make any difference."

"Really? I saw quite a few people demonstrating here the other day. In fact I think I read in the paper that most of the French are opposed to them."

"Don't you worry about that," Sylvie Le Goff replied. Her patronising tone made it clear that this matter was nothing to do with *les Anglais* in Louennec. "It's the prefect who decides. And you, Madame? Are you enjoying your baking?"

"Yes. It's very challenging. I'm looking forward to opening my *boulangerie* in the New Year. It's a beautiful day, isn't it?"

From the corner of her eye, Pippa saw Jennifer's red hatchback approach from the direction of Carhaix, and turned to wave at her. But Jennifer was talking to Luke in the passenger seat and didn't see her. Mariam was in the back, staring out of the window, her face expressionless.

Mme Le Goff had turned to leave but Pippa said, "Excuse me, I just overheard a disturbing incident in the house over there." She gestured towards the white-painted fence and quickly explained what she'd heard and seen.

"You want me to do something about it?" said Mme Le Goff with genuine incomprehension.

"I thought, maybe mention to the police or something? I mean the old woman is clearly being threatened by her stepsons."

Mme Le Goff shrugged. "Everyone in the village knows about that family. What do you expect? There's nothing anyone can do because they all inherited a share of the house, and the widow has the right to live there until her death. Unless they sell the property, or one buys out the others, they're stuck."

With a final "pff" signifying that she already had enough to do, Mme Le Goff said goodbye and walked across the gravel to her car. Pippa wondered whether she should have asked her about the two deaths in the village. If it was really true she knew where the bodies were buried, she might have shed light on what had happened to Adam and Didier, she thought to herself with a smile.

She watched her drive off before picking up her kit and walking the few yards back to her house, still thinking about what she'd just heard. She wasn't going to leave it there.

CHAPTER 15: THE GATHERING STORM

Jennifer put down the mac and cheese in the centre of the kitchen table and returned with a plate of braised cabbage.

"Good game?" she asked Jonathan who had changed for dinner.

"I need to work on my drive," he said. "I think I might ask the pro for a lesson. Derek has really improved his technique."

He sat down and began serving the portions onto each plate, handing the first to Luke.

"*J'aime pas ça*," said Luke, pouting.

"What don't you like? Mac and cheese is one of your favourite things," said Jennifer, in English. They watched as Luke pushed the vegetable to the side of his plate.

"*Je t'ai déjà dit que j'aime pas ça*," he repeated. In recent weeks, he'd taken to replying in French whenever he was addressed in English, which never failed to grate on Jonathan's nerves.

"Luke, I've told you before, when we're at home, we speak English," said Jonathan. "It's our home-grown cabbage and if you don't want to eat now, you can go to your room. We're going out tonight and the babysitter will be here in a minute."

"Where are you going?" Mariam asked. But before either of her parents could reply, Luke had pushed away his chair and headed for the stairs. Jonathan put down the serving spoon with a bang.

"Honestly!" he exclaimed.

Jennifer reached across the table, and mumbled, "Never mind, he can have something else to eat when we've gone out."

"But that's my point," Jonathan grumbled. "I don't understand why you're spoiling him."

"Spoiling him? I'm not spoiling him!"

Jennifer was aware of Mariam observing them in silence. Was she embarrassed or reproving? Jennifer picked up the serving spoon and gave the three of them a portion. They ate in haste and Jonathan looked at his watch before Mariam and Jennifer had finished.

"Look we'd better go," he said. "There'll be something to eat when we get to Derek's."

"Just give us a minute," said Jennifer. "Mariam are you OK to do the washing-up? You don't mind taking care of your little brother until the babysitter gets here, do you?"

Mariam pushed the rest of her food to the edge of her plate, got up, and said: "He's not my brother."

Jennifer gasped. Jonathan stood up. "Mariam, go to your room," he said. "You're talking nonsense. Just what is the matter with you both at the moment?"

Without a word, Mariam went upstairs too. They heard her bedroom door shutting. Jennifer ran up after her.

"Mariam, open up! Let me in," she cried, twisting the door handle but it was locked.

"Come on," Jonathan hissed, as he joined her. "We'll be late."

"How can we leave now? Can't you see she's upset?"

"Yes of course I can. But she'll calm down. Luke's here and they'll be fine."

Jonathan's reaction made her all the more determined to stay.

"You don't get it do you?" she said in a whisper, afraid that Mariam might be listening from the other side of the door.

"Look, she's better now. Everyone says so."

"*Everyone?* Who's *everyone?*"

Jonathan moved towards her but she pushed him away. She stared at him as though he were a stranger before stepping back from the brink. "Right, well you go and sort out Luke," she said eventually. "You started this."

He walked along the corridor and she heard Luke's voice broken by sobs, accusing his father of treating him unfairly.

After a few minutes, Jonathan emerged. Jennifer was still leaning on the wall beside Mariam's bedroom door.

"It's fine," he said. "Luke's coming down for some ice cream." Jennifer knocked gently on the door. "We'll be at Derek's, for the panto. Ring me if you need anything."

"OK." The sound was muffled, but at least it was a reply.

Jennifer and Jonathan went back downstairs and collected their coats. When the car creeped out along the drive, she looked up and saw the silhouette of Mariam standing by the bedroom window.

"You and I need to talk," she told Jonathan.

CHAPTER 16: A REHEARSAL

A swaying lantern lit the porch of Derek and Solenn's stone house on the river bank.

The chill in the air matched the atmosphere in the car. Neither Jennifer nor Jonathan had spoken on the short drive through the village. When they stepped out onto the gravel they could hear a faint trickling noise through the trees below them.

Jonathan knocked and Derek came to the door.

"Sorry we're late," said Jonathan. "Family crisis."

"Don't worry, come in, come in. It's cold out."

Solenn came to greet them and ushered them through the dining room, where a table was piled high with food, into a spacious living room. They waved to the others.

"I'm afraid we're last. So sorry," Jennifer said to Solenn.

"Don't worry, I just got here," Pippa called out from a corner.

The chairs stood in a semicircle leaving space in front of a double bi-fold window which looked over a patio and a grassy garden bathed in lamplight. A piano stood against the wall.

"So, what's your poison?" Derek asked. He poured them each a glass of red wine before saying, "I was just telling the others, the Hairy Biker can't make it tonight. Meredith is coming but won't be here till later. It seems he had an emergency council meeting. It's all about that wind farm business."

Jennifer caught Jonathan's eye and frowned at him as though to say, *Why are we here, then?* But the others were settled with their drinks. Mark, his face slightly flushed, had a bottle placed on the floor next to his chair as usual.

Derek noticed Jennifer's displeasure.

"Anyway," he said, "Look, Jennifer, we decided that as we don't have the director and author present, we could show you some of the props and costumes that Solenn has sourced, so that we don't waste time. And I can play you all a couple of the songs. Is that OK with everyone?"

"But do have something to eat first," said Solenn. They all stood up and followed her into the dining room, where they helped themselves to the nibbles.

"Everything all right?" Pippa asked Jennifer in a low voice. "You don't seem like your usual self."

"Oh, I'm fed up with you know who," she replied. "And I think all this stuff with Mariam is getting to me."

Pippa gave her arm a sympathetic squeeze. "Well, try and enjoy tonight," she said before moving towards a plate of shrimp canapés. "This should be fun, particularly if Craig's not here."

Jennifer grinned and joined Solenn at the table where she was cutting up an entire Brie.

"Did you buy this on the market?" she asked.

"Yes, from Philippe," said Solenn. "I always go there."

"Yes, so do I, but cheese costs as much as meat these days, doesn't it?"

She grimaced in agreement. Jennifer admired Solenn's necklace and matching bracelet featuring the Celtic triskele. "I haven't seen you on the market, lately? Are these the ones that you sell there?"

"Yes. My Breton designs do quite well in the tourist season, but I also sell online. I probably won't be back on the market until Christmas."

She smiled before adding, "I still need my office job, you see."

"Did you ever tell me where you met Derek?" Jennifer took a slice of the cheese and watched as the creamy centre slid out. "This Brie is perfect, by the way."

Solenn smiled at the compliment and replied, "We met at a Breton dancing class in Louennec."

"That sounds like fun! No wonder you both keep so fit," said Jennifer.

Solenn waved one hand before saying, "Oh, Derek is *le sportif*, I don't do anything sporty in particular."

Then she excused herself, saying she had to collect the costumes from upstairs. As she turned away, Jennifer's eyes worked their way up from the finely turned ankle, to the slim hips and pert breasts between which the triskele dangled. The cliché about French women not getting fat had been confirmed once again. Just then, a piano chord rang out. Derek was calling them to the rehearsal. His back was erect on the piano stool, but his body relaxed as he stretched out his fingers and riffed along the entire keyboard to attract their attention.

"This is Mother Goose's song, at the beginning, when the evil landlord has evicted her." He played a few chords before turning towards them to sing:

"I'm old Mother Goose, and I must leave my hoose
Because I'm so poor that I can't afford juice.
My hair is too short, my legs are too long,
And that's why I'm having to sing you this song.
I've got so fat that I can't feed the cat, so what am I to do?
I've got no money to feed my son Billy, so what am I to do?"

Derek winked at Jonathan and they all applauded when he finished.

"So could you manage that, Jonathan?" he asked. "I'm still working on a chorus."

"It's certainly catchy enough," Jonathan replied.

"This song is fattist," Pippa protested but everybody laughed.

Derek said, "Come on, Pippa, it's a panto."

"And Jonathan's not fat, anyway," Jennifer called out.

"Ah well, Solenn is finishing a costume for him that will fill him out."

Jonathan groaned.

Solenn came down the stairs with a bright yellow dress which stuck out from the waist.

"Will this do? I think it will fit you with a cushion inside."

Jonathan looked across at Jennifer, shaking his head.

"Why oh why did I agree to do this?"

"Do you want to try the costume on now?" Solenn asked. Jonathan got up and held it up in front of him.

"You'll look fab in that," said Pippa, grinning. "And what about my costume?"

"Wait," said Solenn. She went back upstairs and returned with a pile of things.

"Here's yours," she said to Pippa.

She held up a heavy white dress. Then she picked up a basket of yellow tennis balls and handed it to Pippa.

"What's that for?"

"They're your golden eggs," said Derek.

"I hope I'm not supposed to lay them on stage . . ." Pippa caught Jennifer's eye and they burst out laughing.

The doorbell rang and a few moments later Meredith swept in, making a dramatic entrance behind Solenn and apologising for being late. She was limping slightly. Emma went to her mother's side, looking concerned.

"I'm so sorry," said Meredith. "I probably shouldn't be here. I've had a flare-up of gout but here I am. I didn't want to disappoint everybody, particularly as Craig couldn't make it."

"You're just in time," Solenn said to her. "Come and have some food. I found you a magic wand."

She dug out a feather duster from her pile and held it up for inspection. Meredith smiled her approval.

"Brilliant, *chérie*," said Derek.

"What's this about Craig's emergency meeting?" Derek asked Meredith.

"Oh, I think there are tensions with the mayor. Sounds like he's trying to get Craig to cool his opposition to the wind farm project. Too vocal, you know?" She added, "But never mind, let's not allow that to spoil our evening. Craig can stand up for himself."

The players spent the next hour trying on the costumes and going through the props. Mark returned to the buffet where he eyed the leftovers.

Jennifer found herself standing next to Derek, who was watching Pippa prancing round the room in her Priscilla costume.

"How was the golf this afternoon?" Jennifer asked him by way of conversation.

"Golf?"

"Yes. Weren't you playing with Jonathan?"

"Oh. No, actually, we didn't play today." He moved away quickly, and picked up a napkin. "Let me just grab the last of the canapés, if Mark has left any. Delicious, aren't they?"

Jennifer realised she was crushing a paper napkin in her hand as the truth dawned on her. She could no longer ignore her suspicions about Jonathan and Emma. How could she have been such a fool? She wondered whether everyone knew and were laughing at her behind her back.

Derek clapped his hands and said, "Shall we finish up here, everyone?" He brandished a rifle.

"This is for the scene where Mother Goose returns from the pool having had a makeover. The Demon King persuaded her to hand over Priscilla in exchange. But in the end she's so bad tempered that she loses her friends, and miserable without Priscilla, so she decides to kill the Demon King to get Priscilla back. Don't worry, it's not loaded," he said, handing it to Jonathan.

"I'm afraid it's a rifle because that's what they mostly use for hunting round here. I've borrowed it from a local farmer."

Jonathan examined it before raising it to his shoulder and pointing it at Pippa.

"Bang, bang," he said.

"Quaaack," she said, sinking to the floor.

They all laughed.

It was getting late and they were all slightly woozy.

"We must go." Jennifer touched Jonathan on the arm. She could see that Solenn and Derek were getting tired. "Anyone need a lift?"

The group began picking up their things and she walked out to the car where she eased herself into the passenger seat. Jonathan followed behind, after escorting Emma to her car.

After they set off down the lane, Jennifer stared straight ahead while marshalling her words in her mind. Eventually, she took a deep breath and said, "The game's up, Jonathan. It's her or me."

"What on earth are you talking about?"

"I know all about your little white lies about playing golf while you're playing away. I don't know whether you've noticed but your children are badly in need of a father right now!"

She jumped as the car drove over a pothole in the lane. "Sorry," he said.

"Sorry for what?" she said, trying not to shout. "For deceiving me and letting down your family?"

"Look, calm down." He stretched out a hand towards her. She pushed it away.

"It's Emma, isn't it?"

"What? I don't know what you're talking about," he insisted. "If you're suggesting that Emma and I are having an affair, you're completely wrong!"

She recoiled, not knowing whether to believe his denial. She watched the glow of the car headlights on the autumn leaves scattered across the lane leading to their house. She remembered her little exchange with Derek and knew that she had to face the painful truth, whatever Jonathan said.

"So what was all that about, just now?" she said.

"What?"

"Your tender farewell with Emma . . ."

"For goodness' sake, Jennifer. Don't be ridiculous. We were just talking about me picking up Romy."

She sat in resentful silence until the car came to a halt. Was he gaslighting her?

"All right," she said, as he switched off the engine. "I'll just say one more thing. Mariam and Luke don't deserve this, they don't deserve hearing us row like they just did, they must suspect what's going on. It's your choice if you want to throw our marriage away. But as of tonight you're sleeping on the sofa!"

And with that, she got out of the car and slammed the door.

CHAPTER 17: THE OLD WOMAN

Pippa loaded the car with her pastries for the market and placed two steaming containers of chicken biryani and rice into the boot.

At least the cooking had distracted her from the troubling events in Louennec. But as she left the house and was about to get into the car, she saw Yann shutting his front door, and the murders were back on her mind.

"Morning," she called out. He raised a hand and walked towards the low box hedge which separated their properties.

"What are you taking to the market today?" he asked, pointing to her open car boot.

"Chicken biryani. It's not spicy and people seem to like it."

He smiled. "Delicious," he said.

Might this be a hint? She thought. An opportunity to invite him round to taste the dish?

"By the way . . ." she called out as he turned towards his car. "Tell me, have there been any developments in the investigation into Adam's murder? Our little community is wondering whether we're being targeted . . ."

Yann stopped and turned back to her, stroking his smooth-shaven jaw. He seemed to hesitate before deciding to speak. "If you promise to keep this to yourself, I can tell you, but it's important for you to remain silent because we have not yet charged anyone in connection with the estate agent's murder. It seems that, like you suggested, it could be to do with his job. You see, some of the local people resent the fact that the house prices have been pushed up by the number of Britons buying properties in the village."

"I see. But why kill an estate agent?" Pippa found the hypothesis hard to believe.

"Let me just say that we found many phone calls from one villager to your estate agent. He bought a house at a high price from him and it turned out that it required major work after he moved in, underpinning in fact. And so the villager lost all his savings and blamed the estate agent."

"Wow. So it was revenge?"

"It would seem so. But Peeper, I beg you. This must remain between us for now, because we are still gathering the evidence. But the rest of the English community doesn't need to worry."

"And what about that poor young man, Didier? Is there any connection between the two deaths?"

He shook his head. "We don't believe so, no."

"Thank you, Yann."

He smiled and turned to go. She was getting the feeling that she was holding him up, but couldn't help saying, "Excuse me, but there's also something else . . ." She told him about the incident at the old woman's house. "I mean, shouldn't this be reported to the police? She's obviously being abused by her family," she said. "But Madame Le Goff told me there's nothing to be done."

"She's right. The whole country suffers from our ridiculous inheritance law. What do you want to do about it? Did you witness the abuse yourself?" She could see he was growing impatient.

"No," she said. *But she'd heard it.*

"So you don't really know what went on there," he said. "The best thing to do would be to convince the woman to file a complaint herself."

Pippa pulled a face. "Well, I must say that's a rather bureaucratic reply. I'm worried that one of these days something worse could happen to her. And then it will be too late."

She knew that Yann didn't need her to tell him how to do his job. But she didn't give him enough time to reply. She pushed down the car boot, got into the driver's seat and watched him return to his car.

That's done it, she thought.

CHAPTER 18: MARKET DAY

Pippa was already waiting for Jennifer at the Central Café after she packed up her market stall.

"Guess what I found out this morning?" said Pippa, her eyes wide with excitement, even before they'd ordered their coffees.

Instead of responding straight away, Jennifer sighed.

"Look. I need to tell you something first . . . Jonathan is cheating on me!" She took out a tissue from her coat pocket and dabbed her eyes. "Sorry."

Pippa reached across the table and squeezed her hand.

"What's happened?" She had a mounting sense of dread that she already knew the answer.

"Did you know he plays golf with Derek from time to time? Well, I found out that he was using that as an excuse to spend time with his mistress on Saturday afternoons. And maybe during the week, for all I know."

"Oh no! Have you confronted him about it?"

"Yes. After the evening at Derek's the other night. He denies it, of course . . . Anyway, I think it's Emma," said Jennifer.

Pippa looked at her friend. She felt awkward. Should she confirm her suspicions?

"I'm sorry," she said, after a moment. "That's so shit."

They both fell silent while the waiter took their order. Jennifer's eyes clouded over.

"Classic, isn't it? Younger woman, midlife crisis . . . I suppose I thought that by moving here the problems in our marriage would disappear. But in fact we're having a meltdown . . ." Her voice trembled, and she dabbed her eyes again. "And I'm worried about the impact on the children. They must have noticed the tension between us . . ."

"Mmm . . . I imagine that's bad timing, what with Mariam."

"Yes. We need to put up a united front, which is difficult enough. Jonathan's not as sympathetic as he could be. He's the sort of person who tells you to get a grip, you know?"

Pippa patted her hand. "How long have you two known each other?"

"Oh, for ever. Since school. We were in the school play together, *The Taming of the Shrew*."

"And you played Kate?"

"Yes, I did! And he was a dashing Petruchio. Then we kept in touch when we went to university and got back together when we were working in London. We tried for a baby for a long time before deciding to adopt. And then of course after Mariam came along, we weren't even trying when I became pregnant with Luke."

"That's often the way, I hear," said Pippa. She leaned back while the waiter placed their coffees in front of them. The café was beginning to fill up with customers looking for tables. Pippa noticed Philippe from the cheese stall looking across at them from the bar and gave him a wave. He held up his glass of red wine in acknowledgement.

"Say cheese," Pippa said to Jennifer who put on a smile automatically before realising what she meant. Philippe had turned back to his mates from the market.

"But tell me. How's Mariam doing?" Pippa added.

Jennifer screwed up her nose. "It's hard to tell, really. She obviously doesn't want to talk about it to us. We're trying to play it cool. Non-judgemental, you know." Her smile was wan.

"I'm sure that's the best way," said Pippa.

"The school head impresses me, and she told me she's dealt with the bullying issue. Jonathan and I looked into changing schools, but we didn't feel like disrupting her schooling again. And the only place round here she could have gone to is a private Catholic school, which didn't feel appropriate to us."

"Gosh. I'm sure she'll get through this. Kids are resilient at that age. Did you think about going back to London?"

"Yes, we did. But we decided that it would be an even bigger disruption for the family to go back after only a year here. I mean we need to give ourselves a chance to make this work, rather than give up at the first hurdle, don't you think? Without mentioning the financial aspect." She winced. "I mean, we sold our place in London to come here, and after that how do we get back into that market?"

She lapsed into silence and drained her espresso before adding, "Anyway, maybe all this is irrelevant. Who knows if Jonathan and I even have a future now?" She crumpled the tissue and stuffed it into her jeans pocket. "Look, I'm sorry for burdening you with my problems."

"I'm here for you, Jennifer," Pippa said.

Jennifer sat up straight and wiped away a rogue tear with her hand. "We'd better go. But first tell me what you found out this morning."

She gestured to the waiter to bring their bill. Pippa recounted her conversation with Yann and finished with a warning to Jennifer not to tell anybody. "I've been sworn to secrecy. And what's more, Yann admitted that I was right to have suggested that Adam might have been killed because he was an estate agent. I told him that back home, estate agents and journalists have terrible reputations."

"Really?" said Jennifer. "I hadn't heard that. Maybe Craig will be next!"

They both smiled before Pippa said, "But I should have asked him about how the killer knew that Adam was at your place."

Jennifer knitted her brow while she reflected. "Do you think the murderer had an accomplice? Someone who saw his car parked outside our place?"

Pippa gripped Jennifer's arm. "Exactly! But who?"

"There's a farmer who goes past the house on his tractor at the same time every night. But we wouldn't have heard him that evening because we were in the back. He might have tipped off the killer . . . I'll see if I can find out the farmer's name."

"But hang on," said Pippa. "They could have killed Adam at home, couldn't they?"

"It depends," said Jennifer. "It might have been a spur-of-the-moment thing. Do you know where he lived?"

Pippa gestured in the direction of the market. "Over there, on the other side of the market, there's a little block of flats." She screwed up her nose. "But wouldn't they have video on the entrance, that sort of thing? It would be much easier to catch him like they did in the middle of nowhere."

Jennifer nodded.

"Yann also said they don't think there was any connection between Adam's death and Didier," Pippa went on.

"That's good. Or is it? I mean one killer is bad enough. But didn't Craig say he saw two people push Didier into the slurry?"

Jennifer looked up at two people who were standing right beside their table.

"Let's pay," she murmured. She wrapped her scarf round her neck while Pippa dug into her handbag for her purse, in order to leave some small change as a tip.

As they got up, Pippa laid a reassuring hand on Jennifer's arm. "You know you can call me any time."

CHAPTER 19: A DONATION

Pippa was the last to arrive for the panto rehearsal at Craig and Meredith's the following week. The dog barked but for once remained inside his kennel without coming out to tackle her.

The living room had been cleared to make space in front of the fireplace, where ruby embers glistened. Pippa waved to everyone, and instinctively moved to stand next to Jennifer.

"Help yourselves, everyone," said Meredith, gesturing towards the dining table where the usual finger food and wine that accompanied their panto evenings was laid out.

Mark piled his plate high with sandwiches and found a seat at the back of the room next to a bottle of wine that he'd appropriated.

Derek and Solenn, inseparable as ever, stood in the opposite corner munching on sticks of celery. Pippa noticed Jonathan in a group with Emma and her parents.

"How's it going?" she asked Jennifer quietly, with a glance in Jonathan's direction.

Jennifer pulled a face. "He's still sleeping on the sofa, if that's what you mean," she said. "I told the children that it's because he snores."

"Does he?"

"No."

They turned their backs to the others to spread some pâté onto slices of baguette.

"I'm angry now," said Jennifer. "I'm moving on from being upset."

"What are you two conspirators plotting?" Meredith suddenly cut in.

"Pippa's bringing me up to date on her bakery plans," said Jennifer quickly.

Without missing a beat, Pippa said, "Would you believe that I've had a donation of five hundred euros from an anonymous donor on the fundraising site?"

"Gosh that's fantastic," said Meredith. "Any idea who it is?"

Pippa shook her head. "It could be one of my friends from home, but I've not found out yet for sure."

She drifted away and decided to engage Mark in conversation. But just as she was about to say the first thing that came into her head, Craig clapped his hands to get their attention. Mark looked round and put down his plate.

"Right everyone. I hope you've all learned your script, because this is absolutely the last chance before the dress rehearsal in the village hall. Derek, I'm sorry, there's no piano here, but everyone knows their songs, so we'll just muddle through regardless. I'll prompt as necessary."

He picked up the script from his desk in the corner. "Act one, Scene one. Come on Jonathan and Pippa, you're on!"

CHAPTER 20: A NEW FRIEND

It was Jennifer's turn to do the afternoon school run two days later.

"Can Pervenche come to tea, Mum?" Mariam asked. She gestured to a long-legged blonde girl behind her. "Her mum says it's OK."

"Hop in," Jennifer said from the driving seat of the hatchback. "*Bonjour*, Pervenche. Sorry it's grubby in the back." It was the first time she'd seen Mariam with a schoolfriend since the beginning of the school year. Luke, in the passenger seat beside her, seemed as surprised as she was.

"*Bonjour*, Madame," said Pervenche. She flashed a gap-toothed smile in Jennifer's direction.

"That's a nice name, Pervenche," said Jennifer. "Not a Breton name?"

"It means periwinkle," said Mariam. She pushed some plastic bags onto the floor to make room for the two of them.

"My parents came from Paris and moved to Carhaix," said Pervenche, catching Jennifer's eye in the rear mirror from the back seat. "My dad's involved in organising the rock festival here."

"He can get us free tickets to the *Vieilles Charrues*," said Mariam. "The Arctic Monkeys are headlining at the festival next summer!"

Jennifer stopped off at a *boulangerie* in Carhaix to pick up a baguette plus a tart that the girls could share as a treat. By the time they got home, it was almost dark. The red lights of the wind farm on the crest of the hill across the valley blinked at them in the clear November air. When they came to a halt outside the house, she presumed Jonathan must still be working upstairs. Luke took his school backpack up to his room.

"Remember, only half an hour playing your video game. Haven't you got homework to do?" Jennifer called up to him on the staircase. He turned round to glare at her.

"After dinner," he said.

Mariam divided the apple tart into two on the kitchen counter and began eating her portion with her fingers. Pervenche followed suit and they headed towards the front door, leaving Jennifer to clean up the trail of crumbs.

"Mum, is it OK if I show Pervenche the baby rabbits?" Mariam asked on the way out.

"As long as you don't take them out of their cage," she said. Lady Gaga, so christened by Mariam because of her soft white fur, had given birth to six babies three weeks earlier. They were already hopping around in the cage and eating grain and hay. Jennifer worried that the children might get too attached to them when in a few short months they were destined to be sent to market.

She checked the henhouse, where she found more eggs in the nesting boxes, and gave more hay to the sheep while the girls were with the rabbits. When she returned to the house, Jonathan was downstairs with Luke and had found something in the freezer for supper.

They'd finished eating by eight o'clock and Jonathan offered to take Pervenche home. Jennifer went upstairs to find Mariam whose bedroom door was open. She was bent over her computer.

"Pervenche seems nice," she said, softly. "So she's in your class?"

Mariam turned round and nodded. She looked so stern with her wire-rimmed glasses.

"She's like us," she said.

"What do you mean?"

"An outsider. They don't like Parisians here, do they?"

Jennifer laughed. That was so true. "I don't think anyone outside Paris likes Parisians. But you know you can always bring any of your friends home," she added. "I mean it's great that you're seeing friends in real life." She put air quotes around the last three words.

"Don't worry, Mum, it's OK," said Mariam. Jennifer approached her and gave her a hug.

"So are things better at school now? You know you can talk to us about your feelings, don't you?"

"I said, don't worry, didn't I?" said Mariam.

Jennifer took that to mean yes and went back downstairs, reassured.

CHAPTER 21: "HE'S BEHIND YOU!"

Craig clapped his hands. The sound echoed from the stage of the village hall where the Louennec players had gathered, ready for the dress rehearsal.

They were counting down to the big night. Craig had ensured there was a poster outside the *mairie* advertising the panto, and he'd done an interview with *Le Télégramme* for which Jennifer had taken a photo of the troupe in costume. Craig had done his best to explain the pantomime tradition to the reporter but the paper had reduced his hour-long interview to a picture caption. The paper's French readers were not the target audience for an English farce.

"Come on everyone, we've not got all night." He turned to Meredith, who was in net curtains, belted at the waist, with a tiara on her head.

"Don't forget to hit video on your phone for the performance. And are you OK to prompt, if need be?"

"But I'm Fairy Nuff," she said, waving her feather duster.

Craig seemed flustered. "You can do it. You've only got a small part and you wrote the script anyway."

"Yes, dear. Don't worry. It'll be fine," she soothed.

"Where's Jonathan? You're on, Mother Goose. Lights!"

Jonathan picked his way to the front and up the steps to the stage. His padded yellow dress, hobnail boots and a dark wig with ringlets had transformed him for the part. Solenn had gone to town as make-up artist and he was disfigured by pencilled wrinkles.

"Is anyone going to do the audience participation? Get us in the mood?" he asked.

Craig, dressed in his Demon King costume consisting of a loose shirt and breeches held up with braces, pointed to a couple of rows of seats at the back of the hall where the players could sit. He had on a feathered hat and looked more like an Austrian yodeller than pantomime villain.

"At the back," he said. "And I've left the door open so if anyone wanders in they can shout out too. Or applaud. So don't get put off your lines. This is your last chance."

Derek struck up a tune on the piano, and they were off.

* * *

Craig was in his element. So far the dress rehearsal had gone without a hitch. Nobody had forgotten their lines, and they seemed to be enjoying themselves. He was master of ceremonies, director and actor all rolled into one. By the time the interval came, his shirt was drenched in sweat.

He clapped his hands again for attention. "Look everyone. I've scheduled a fifteen-minute interval now but what about carrying on? Everyone OK with that?"

Nobody objected. Pippa, playing Priscilla, and Jonathan, stayed on stage. Solenn had found a gold conical party hat which Pippa had secured with its elastic behind her head to form a beak. She was resplendent in her white flared dress. The other players moved to the back, some sitting on the chairs. Some curious villagers were standing behind them by the open door.

Craig had his nose in the script. "Right. Now this is where Mother Goose comes back from the magic pool after giving Priscilla to the Demon King in return for wealth and beauty. Ready?"

"Aren't you supposed to be onstage as well, Craig? The Demon King has got hold of Priscilla," said Meredith.

"Yes, yes, I'm just coming," Craig replied. "Derek, we're ready for you."

Derek pressed a few gloomy chords on the piano in front of the stage and Jonathan entered. He'd removed the cushion from inside his dress, which was now belted tightly around the waist. The dark wrinkles had been wiped from his face, and his costume scattered with glitter. Pippa gave a couple of soft quacks indicating that she didn't recognise the glamorous new Mother Goose.

Jonathan gave a twirl, and began singing in a low growl. *"The magic pool, the magic pool, gave me the secret of eternal yoof."* He sat down at his kitchen table and explained how miserable he was. *"But now I'm home, I'm all alone and miss my Priscilla the egg-laying goose."*

Pippa quacked loudly as a rope around her neck was tugged. Craig stood at the other side of the stage, holding the other end.

"Oh my best friend Priscilla, I miss you, I'm so wretched without you," Jonathan wailed. Pippa waddled around the stage, forced to follow her new master.

Somebody at the back started hissing, and others began booing Craig who was waving his arms around impatiently.

"Shut up you lot," he said to the small audience. "I'm in charge of the goose who lays the golden eggs now!"

"Oh no you're not," someone said.

"Oh yes I am," he insisted, louder. He could hear the laughter from the back. This was going better than expected.

Jonathan stepped forward, his ringlets quivering. "Oh no, you're not! You're a cruel and evil man and you manipulated me. I've got another idea." He went back to the kitchen table and picked up the rifle.

He walked to the front and brandished the weapon. "Shall I?" he asked. There was a low murmur from the spectators. "I can't hear you!" he said. "I said, shall I?"

"Yes!" the audience screamed. Someone shouted, "He's behind you!" and Jonathan turned to face Craig, with the rifle pointed straight at him. There was a loud popping noise and Craig fell to the floor. A ripple of applause could be heard as some of the players admired his acting skills as the Demon King. But Pippa screamed. She rushed across the stage and fell to her knees next to Craig, whose shirt was stained by a red flower of blood.

"Call an ambulance!" she cried out.

CHAPTER 22: CRAIG

For a moment, no one else moved and then panic ensued. Only Jonathan stood in silent bewilderment, holding the gun.

Meredith paced up and down on the phone to the emergency services with tears streaming down her cheeks. She kept repeating, "Where are they?"

Derek rushed onto the stage and began attempting to revive Craig. Emma followed him up the steps, pushing Pippa aside. As she passed Jonathan, she said in a stage whisper, "I'll never forgive you if you've killed my father."

Pippa got up. Her white frock was stained with bright red blood. "Put that down," she said to Jonathan. "Nobody should touch it."

He moved back to the table and left the rifle there. Jennifer ran onto the stage to Jonathan to comfort him.

"What happened?" he said. "I can't believe it." His body was shaken by sobs which caused glitter to fall from his dress onto the floor.

Two paramedics came into the hall and went onto the stage to tend to Craig. Derek stepped back, his hands and shirt stained with blood. Jennifer could tell from the look on their faces that Craig's condition was grave. One of them went out and came back with a stretcher while the other one examined Craig. Moments later the sound of a police car siren could be heard and two gendarmes burst in, surveying the scene from the door.

"What's going on here?" one of them asked.

"It's a pantomime," said Pippa, removing her golden beak.

"*Un quoi?*"

She explained that it involved dressing up and lots of jokes and was "*typiquement anglais*".

"And how do you spell that?" asked one, writing in his notebook. The other had gone up to the stage where the paramedics had hauled Craig onto the stretcher.

The village hall was now a crime scene.

* * *

The mood changed abruptly in Louennec after Craig's death. The villagers had been preparing to celebrate Christmas, buying festive decorations, cutting down mistletoe and swapping recipes at the market in Carhaix. But now they spoke in hushed tones about "*les Anglais*" when they bumped into acquaintances in the market square, sheltering under umbrellas from the December rain. The news had travelled round the village at the speed of light and, according to the rumour amplified by the lack of hard facts, the finger of guilt pointed at Jonathan.

Two days after the shooting, Jennifer picked up the local paper which highlighted the fact that it was the third murder in the village in a matter of months. A full page devoted to Louennec described the gendarmes arriving at the hall to discover a woman dressed as a goose, a man dressed as a woman, and a man in short trousers covered in blood, lying on the stage.

It was swiftly established that the fatal shot had not been fired by Jonathan, because the rifle wasn't loaded. The prosecutor had launched an investigation into suspected murder by X. That meant they didn't have a clue as to the murderer's identity. The tearful widow was quoted as saying that she had no idea who would have killed her husband.

So, at the village café, on the street, and in the privacy of their homes there was only one question on the lips of all the villagers, Bretons and Britons alike: whodunnit?

Jonathan spent the next few days mainly upstairs in his office. When Jennifer took him up a cup of tea in the afternoons, she'd found him slumped in his chair gazing at an empty computer screen. One day after Luke had come home from school he'd asked, "Daddy, are you a murderer?" Mariam had remained immured in silence, keeping her feelings to herself, and Jennifer feared another downwards spiral. At least the children had been spared the sight of Craig being shot; they'd decided at the last minute to let them stay at home on the night of the dress rehearsal.

"Do you think the killer was the one who called out 'he's behind you'?" Jonathan asked Jennifer one evening after the children had gone upstairs.

"Who knows?" Jennifer replied. She stopped doing the washing-up in the sink while he continued wiping the dishes with a tea towel. "I think it had to be someone standing at the door."

"Yes, you're right. Do you remember that Craig left the door at the back open, and it's possible that somebody was standing there in the darkness, and then . . . bang."

"Yes. But unless they have the murder weapon, how on earth are they going to find the murderer?" said Jennifer. She hugged Jonathan who put an arm round her waist. The tragedy had somehow brought them closer together. Jennifer felt sorry for him, and had allowed her husband to return to the marital bed. But from her side of the mattress, she considered that he was on probation.

How could she ever trust him again, despite his protestations of innocence? Now was not the time for confrontation, however. In any case, with Emma grieving for her dead father, maybe the tragedy might jolt her into seeing sense. Or on the other hand . . . maybe not. The little that she knew about Emma had marked her out as a predator in Jennifer's mind. She'd heard on the grapevine that Emma's husband divorced her after she briefly pursued a childhood sweetheart via Facebook. How could she be so selfish to ignore the welfare of their small child? How many more lovers had she notched up since arriving in Carhaix?

"At least you're in the clear, that's the main thing," Jennifer reassured Jonathan.

"Yes. The past few days have been the worst of my life. I believed that I'd fired the damn thing. I thought they were going to arrest me when they took me out for questioning. Thank God they let us know so quickly about the rifle." He looked into space, shaking his head.

"And thank God you didn't confess on the spot!" said Jennifer. "Maybe Forensics will come up with a clue to the murderer. I wonder how long they'll keep the hall sealed?"

"Have you spoken to Meredith?" he asked.

"Yes. She's in pieces, of course. I wondered what she was doing about the funeral. She's waiting to get the body back." Jennifer returned to washing the plates.

"Do you know if she cancelled the pantomime?"

"Yes, she said she had. I thought that went without saying," said Jennifer.

"That poor family. Poor Meredith, poor Emma, and poor Romy. What on earth did Craig do to deserve that?"

CHAPTER 23: A VISIT

Jennifer went upstairs in search of the girls.

"Come on, Pervenche, time to go. Your mum will be wondering where you are."

"Just a sec," Mariam said. The bedroom door opened and Jennifer could see Pervenche sitting on the bed, waving her hands in the air. Mariam and Pervenche had painted their nails with bright pink varnish.

"I'll wait in the car," Jennifer said.

A few minutes later, Pervenche appeared, a tote bag over her shoulder.

"Do you feel that you've settled in now?" Jennifer asked as they set off towards Carhaix.

Pervenche pulled down her lips. "So-so," she replied.

"They've not been teasing you in the playground as well, have they?" she asked, turning to face her as she drove. The windscreen wipers punctuated their conversation in the drizzle.

"No. Just Mariam," Pervenche said after a beat.

Jennifer saw her opportunity. "And who is the girl who does this?"

Pervenche hesitated for a second, as though weighing the consequences of her reply, then said, "Maelie." The name had a Breton ring to it.

"Maelie who?" Jennifer tried to sound as natural as possible.

"She's stopped it now."

"That's good. I thought so. But what's her name?"

"Maelie Seznec." The name wasn't familiar. But Jennifer didn't know the last names of any of the mothers who gathered by the school gates. Pervenche glanced out of the window as though she feared being struck dead by a thunderbolt. Jennifer reached over and patted the girl's hand as she drove.

"Pervenche, don't worry. Everything will be fine. You know that you can trust me, don't you? I just want Mariam to be happy, and you're a good friend."

* * *

Jennifer checked the time after she dropped Pervenche at her house. She parked by the side of the road and took out her phone. Spurred on by adrenalin, she was able to quickly trace the Seznec family to a village a short distance from Louennec.

About fifteen minutes later, she pulled up outside a white-painted modern house with two cars parked outside. She swallowed nervously.

She rang the doorbell and a teenage boy with a bad case of acne opened the door.

"*Bonjour*, is your mother in?" Jennifer asked with a smile.

She heard him shout "Maman!" before disappearing inside, leaving the door ajar.

A woman with a helmet of dark hair and a small, mean-looking mouth came to the door. They recognised each other immediately: Mme Seznec was one of Jennifer's customers on the market.

Her brain whirred. She decided to press on with her plan. She'd prepared a little speech and had checked the vocabulary to avoid making grammar mistakes. She cleared her throat before saying, "Madame Seznec, you have a daughter, Maelie, do you not?"

The woman seemed confused as to why this was of interest to her chicken seller. But she nodded that she did.

"OK, well, it has been brought to my attention that Maelie has been bullying my daughter at school, and this has had a very serious effect on her. Her studies have suffered because of this. I'm not going to go into details as to what happened in the school yard but I can tell you that Maelie used racist and sectarian language which upset my daughter."

"Racist, Madame?" Mme Seznec's voice was shrill. "And why would she use such language against your daughter?"

"Because she has Somalian heritage, that's why, and she looks different from the other pupils." Jennifer wondered whether she'd already said too much. She didn't want to get into a slanging match with this customer.

But then she couldn't help adding, "And in the light of this unfortunate situation, Madame, I'm afraid that I don't wish you to buy any chickens from me again!"

With that, she turned on her heel, and walked back to the car in the drizzle while summoning as much dignity as she could muster. Out of the corner of her eye, she saw the door slam shut.

Oh dear, she thought, *I've made my first enemy in the commune.*

CHAPTER 24: A CEREMONY

The hearse pulled up outside the village church in a short sharp shower so frequent in the Breton winter.

The four pallbearers staggered slightly as they hoisted Craig's coffin onto their shoulders. Meredith entered the church behind them, clutching Emma's arm as the organist played a dirge. Both women were dressed in black and stared straight ahead until they reached their front-row pew. Jennifer recognised a short, moustachioed man who sat next to Meredith. It was Mathieu, the mayor of the *commune*, and he was wearing his tricolore sash of office for the event. Jennifer had occasionally taken his picture for *Le Télégramme* at ceremonies in the village hall. Glancing around, she realised that the entire village council must have turned out to pay their respects to their late colleague. She glimpsed Mme Le Goff, also in black, sitting at the back.

Jennifer had organised the printing of the funeral programme by a local photographer in Carhaix, and placed copies on all the pews. A photograph of a younger Craig on his motorbike, recognisable from his bushy eyebrows and fleshy lips, stared out from the front page. But the ceremony was stark in its austerity. There were prayers in French, psalms and two hymns. Jennifer murmured the Lord's prayer in

English because she didn't know the words in French. She wondered whether Meredith had said anything to the priest about half of the congregation being English. But he didn't seem to have considered making the slightest concession to Craig's friends and family, and his eulogy read like a CV.

The priest described how Craig had started out as a business reporter in London before becoming a sub-editor in Somerset. He noted his membership of the council and his devotion to Meredith and his family but only mentioned in passing his role in the Louennec players.

The ceremony wound up with an invitation to those who wished to take communion to step forward. Suddenly, seemingly emerging out of nowhere, half a dozen elderly villagers dressed in black walked to the front, crossing themselves and kneeling in front of the altar like a silent chorus in a Greek tragedy. Meredith and Emma turned round in their seats, mystified. Jennifer wondered what Meredith must be thinking. But perhaps she was drugged up to the eyeballs and wasn't thinking anything at all.

A procession began to form for the short walk to the small graveyard where granite Breton crosses, covered in moss, stood guard over the dead. The heavens opened again and everyone raised their umbrellas as they left the church. Meredith, again supported by her daughter, took up the lead behind the coffin.

"Well, the priest certainly took the jokes out of that speech," Jennifer commented to Jonathan as they filed out past the village hall whose entrance was no longer scarred by crime scene tape.

"It was quite different from any of the funerals that I've been to in England," said Jonathan.

"Well, it was a Catholic service, and they're very religious here in Brittany, aren't they? Maybe that's what Meredith wanted."

They stood silently beside the grave as the priest consigned Craig to a dark, muddy hole. Meredith, elegant in grief, wiped her eyes discreetly. When it was over, some villagers approached her and shook her hand. "*Mes condoléances*, Madame," they said, one after another. The English contingent took their place in the queue.

When Jennifer and Jonathan reached the front and gave Meredith a hug, she thanked them for coming and said, "The priest was supposed to mention drinks at home for those who want to come, but maybe he forgot. Anyway, anyone's welcome, so spread the word."

"We will, and thanks for the invitation," said Jonathan. "But we won't stay long as we've got to pick up the kids."

"Oh yes, of course," said Meredith. "Emma will have to pick up Romy. We thought it was better that she went to school as usual today. She's too young for all this."

"We can take care of that, don't worry, when we go for Luke," Jennifer offered. She remembered that when she'd dropped him off at school that morning and explained that Craig was being put in a box because he'd died, he'd asked, "When's he coming out?"

Half an hour later, about twenty mourners had reassembled at Meredith's house, crowded into the dining room. Emma brought out baguettes and slices of saucisson and cheese, while Mark, as lugubrious as ever, took care of the drinks, starting with himself.

"I just wanted to say thank you to everyone for your support at this time," said Meredith in French. Then she switched to English. "It's still too raw to say anything else, really, I still can't believe that Craig . . . has gone. I'm sorry, I'd better stop there." Then finally, she added, in French, "If anyone wants to say anything? *Monsieur le maire?*"

Mathieu stepped forward and stood next to Meredith. Speaking in a mixture of French and English, he said, "Marie, we are here today because we have lost a friend." Meredith didn't correct him on either point. "Craig was *un véritable pilier de notre communauté*. As a council member he used all his considerable energy to improve the lives of our villagers and we owe him a great debt." He cleared his throat. "Sadly, he passed away before his work was finished." Raising his glass, he said, "*Je porte un toast à sa mémoire.*"

"Cheers," someone called out in English. They all clinked glasses.

Meredith said to the gathering, "Thank you all for coming, and thank you for your kind words, *Monsieur le maire*."

Jonathan nudged Jennifer. "Shouldn't somebody say something about the panto?"

"You do it," she suggested.

"No, you. Go ahead." He pushed her gently to the front.

Jennifer cleared her throat, and began speaking in French. "Hello everyone. I'm Jennifer. Craig founded the Louennec players, which we joined this year for the annual pantomime. It brought us into your community, and I'm so grateful for that. We now feel that we belong here, and I don't know what we'll do without him." She swallowed hard, starting to feel the emotion welling up. She noticed Meredith wiping away tears.

"Anyway, we'll be here for you, Meredith," she added, in English. Then she raised her glass. "And here's a toast for Craig. He'll be missed."

The tensions subsided. Some of the guests saw an opportunity to leave. Jonathan looked at his watch, signalling to Jennifer that it was time for the school run.

"We're going now," she said to Meredith. "We'll bring Romy back here."

"Thank you," said Meredith. She seemed to have aged in the days since Craig's death.

"Do you want to let Emma know?" Jennifer asked Jonathan.

"No, I'm sure that's fine." He turned to leave.

"See you soon," she said to Meredith. "Let us know if there's anything you need."

CHAPTER 25: THE TURBINE

The small, independent bakery in Carhaix had seemed like an ideal match for Pippa.

But there was just one problem. Two weeks into her apprenticeship she found herself bridling at being given instructions by a motocross fanatic who spent every spare minute in the back room on the phone to his mates. The baker, Loic, was twenty-five and she was old enough to be his mother.

He always gave her a cheery *Bonjour* when she arrived at 9 a.m. She was grateful that he hadn't put her on an earlier shift and he'd already taken care of the first batch of baking by the time she got there. She didn't mind having the extra freedom to take over the back room operations where she laminated croissant doughs and shaped bread loaves. But if she had a question he was nowhere to be seen, so she found herself serving at the till before returning to the back to pick up what she was doing.

She rarely managed lunch because he offered a sandwich service which he expected her to provide. She sat slapping butter onto sliced baguettes while Loic called out the orders from the counter.

"Two tuna tomato salads," or, "One ham and cheese."

On that Tuesday, it was one sandwich too many. She waited until the customer had left the bakery and said to Loic, "Can we have a word?"

He grabbed his packet of cigarettes, and joined her in the back where a pile of baguette dough was ready to be pre-shaped. He pushed open the back door and they stood outside in the cold. He glanced at his phone.

"Loic, would you *please* not do that," she said. He put the phone in his jeans back pocket like a disobedient child.

"Look, I'm sorry, but this isn't working for me," she said. "I think you're treating me very unfairly." Her voice quivered as she added, "It's not an apprentice you need, it's a slave!"

He took a step back in astonishment, bumping into the rubbish bin. He held out his pack of cigarettes to offer her one. Maybe he thought that's all she needed, but she was already taking off her apron.

"So that's it!" she said, handing it to him. He took it in silence. "I'm done. Have a nice day." And summoning all the dignity she could muster, she walked back through the bakery, stopped to help herself to two millefeuilles pastries from the display, which she'd baked earlier, and left without looking back.

* * *

Pippa drove back to Louennec paying hardly any attention to her speed. As she swung off the main road to turn into the village, she glanced up at the turbines on the ridge above. Something had caught her eye. It was a still day, and the blades were motionless. But something — or someone — was hanging from the top of one of them.

She stopped the car and called Jennifer.

"Are you busy?" she asked.

"Not right now, but I've got stuff to do in an hour. Why?"

"You know the wind farm on the hill above the village? I couldn't swear to this as I'm too far away, but I think there's someone hanging from a turbine!"

"Jesus! I'm on my way."

Pippa carried on along a circuitous route which led her to the top of the hill. She saw Jennifer's red car heading towards her from the opposite direction as she reached a lane which ran along the summit. She flashed her headlights in recognition and Jennifer came to a halt. Pippa pulled up beside her and they both rolled down their windows.

"Did you see?" Pippa asked. Jennifer got out of the car, carrying her camera.

"Yes, shall we head up there?" She indicated towards the turbines which were installed in large clearings like gashes on the hilltop, and started walking.

They could see the body swinging gently in the breeze. Pippa could feel her legs begin to shake at the thought of a fourth murder in the village.

"Who is it, do you think?" she asked. "Has he been lynched or what?"

"Well, it seems to be a man, as he's wearing trousers and a jacket. But let's go closer."

They reached the foot of the turbine and looked up. A rope had been swung over the turbine blade and attached round the man's neck.

"How on earth could anyone do that? I mean it's about a hundred feet up, isn't it?" said Jennifer, as she clicked away.

"I think it's higher than that. They must have attached it to the blade when it was lowered, and then it would be hoisted up when it was switched it on. But . . . there's something funny about this."

They stared at the figure outlined against the sky. Then Jennifer exclaimed, "It's not a body! It's too light. It's a blow-up doll! Wait while I zoom in with my camera."

"What?!" Pippa walked round the turbine base for a better look. "You're right. It's like an effigy."

"This is giving me the creeps," she added. "Can you see the face?"

They peered upwards but the face was in the wrong direction. Jennifer went round the other side with her camera before coming back to stand next to Pippa.

"Look at this," she said, showing Pippa a photo which she enlarged with her fingers. "Oh no! Look at the tricolore sash! And he has a moustache."

The two women stared at each other. They'd both identified Mathieu the mayor.

CHAPTER 26: YANN

It was early evening when Pippa returned home, the boot filled with shopping from the supermarket.

She slammed the car door, distracted by the day's turmoil, before she noticed Yann bent over the box hedge with a pair of shears in his hand.

He stood up and waved. "Good evening, Peeper. How are you?"

"Could be better," she said. "I quit my job today."

His face crumpled in sympathy. "I'm so sorry to hear that." He seemed to hesitate before adding, "Come round for a drink later if you want to talk about it?"

She was so touched by the unexpected invitation that she agreed at once. He helped her take the shopping to the door and returned to his hedge trimming.

An hour later, Pippa was dressed in a freshly ironed dress and had put just a trace of eau de toilette behind each ear. She rang the doorbell, realising that it was the first time she'd been invited to Yann's house.

He seemed slightly nervous when he opened the door, and accepted the two slightly battered millefeuilles which she'd rescued from the *boulangerie*. They bumped into each other when he led her along the corridor into his ivory-coloured kitchen which was the exact replica of hers. *This feels like a date*, she thought.

They sat at the kitchen table where he'd set out glasses on a tray.

"I have whisky, gin, martini . . . and Gros Plant," he said.

"The wine will be fine," she said. "I never drink hard liquor."

"Neither do I," he said with a smile. "It's only for guests." He fetched the white wine from the fridge.

He sat down next to her and they clinked glasses.

"So, tell me what happened," he said.

Should she tell him? She cleared her throat. "I walked out because my boss was mean. *Un salaud*." She explained the scene with Loic, and concluded, "So now I've got to find another bakery to finish my course. I need another two months' experience."

"Do you have any ideas?" he asked. "What about one of the villages round here?"

"Yes, I think I'd rather do that, than go back to Carhaix." She frowned. "I might have a bad reputation in town now."

"It strikes me that Loic will have trouble replacing you, given everything you were expected to do," he said.

"Thank you. Actually, I stole the cakes that I brought round tonight. Although, I should add that I was the one who baked them."

He burst out laughing. "So you are a criminal! You should be arrested."

"Maybe you shouldn't even try them, as they're stolen goods," she said. He grinned.

"Do you have plans for dinner? If you want to stay, I can make an omelette and we can have the cakes afterwards."

She studied his face, his dark eyes soft and warm.

"That's kind of you. Yes please," she responded.

Their nervousness evaporated as the wine flowed. Yann rustled up a fluffy omelette and sprinkled it with parsley before placing Pippa's share in front of her.

"Are you staying here for Christmas?" he asked.

"No, I'm going home to see my daughters. What about you?"

"I'm spending Christmas Eve with my mother in Vannes."

"Is that all? Aren't you taking time off?"

Yann shrugged. "Christmas Day is a holiday for me this year but that's it. So I'll drive back to Louennec after lunch. And then back to work the next day."

"England shuts down for at least a week between Christmas and New Year." Pippa grinned. "Although not the police, of course."

"Ah, the British workmen. I heard about that," he said. "We have many days off in May. Much better. At least it's sunny weather."

Pippa felt encouraged to mention the blow-up doll on the turbine blade.

"It was my friend Jennifer who called the *gendarmerie*. And she took pictures," she admitted.

Yann's face expressed surprise, then anger. Finally, he grinned. Knowing how he didn't like what he saw as their interference in police business, Pippa was relieved.

"You two," he said with a shake of the head. "You are amazing. But when the developers find out who did this, I bet they'll sue. This is sabotage."

"It might be sabotage, but whoever did this has a grievance against Mathieu, don't you think?"

"Maybe, maybe not . . . There is the symbolism of the doll resembling him, hanging from the wind turbine," he agreed. "So you can imagine that our enquiries will focus on the protesters."

"Unfortunately, Didier, the leading protester is already dead," Pippa pointed out.

"Yes, unfortunately." Yann's tone of voice indicated that he wanted to shut down the conversation. There was a pause while he cleared away the plates and took out the millefeuilles. They used forks to cut into the golden crispness surrounding the creamy filling.

"Bravo!" said Yann. "It's as good, if not better, than any *pâtisserie* round here."

Pippa felt as though she was bathing in a warm bath full of bubbles, cheered by the compliment. They leaned back in their seats and toasted each other. A second bottle had appeared on the table. She was starting to feel a little tipsy.

"You must miss your friend," said Yann.

"What friend?"

"The one who was killed in the village hall."

"Oh, he wasn't a friend. I was in their amateur dramatic society, that's all. But I haven't seen anything about the investigation except that they don't have a suspect. Do you know what's going on?"

Yann pulled down his lips. "First of all we don't have the murder weapon. Although we know from an analysis of the bullet that it wasn't fired from a rifle. It was a handgun."

"Oh . . . and can you trace it?"

"Peeper, what I'm telling you is in the strictest confidentiality, do you understand?"

She nodded her head vigorously. "Yes, of course."

"We are now checking everyone with a licence in the village, which could take some time. And it could be a weapon bought on the black market. But I think another problem is the motive. Why would anyone want to kill him?"

"Well, what about the turbine issue? People here are very upset about it . . . look at what happened to Didier," she said.

"Yes, of course everyone knows about that in Louennec, but . . . why kill?"

"For the same reason that Didier found himself in the deep end of a slurry tank! Craig said to me after Didier died that he suspected the mayor of being behind it."

"Mathieu?"

"Yes. He showed up at Craig's funeral and made a speech at Meredith's afterwards and I thought that Craig would have been turning in his grave. He couldn't stand him."

"But again, why would the mayor want to kill Didier, or Craig for that matter? And why would he take such a risk as a public official?"

"You're the investigator, you figure it out!" she snapped, before quickly adding, "Sorry."

She looked sideways at him wondering whether this was a good moment, and decided to seize the opportunity.

"By the way, you remember my estate agent, Adam?"

"Of course." He sounded tetchy. But Pippa ploughed on.

"Well, we were thinking that the killer might have had an accomplice. I mean, the killer obviously knew where Adam was on the night of the murder."

Yann said nothing. Pippa couldn't be sure whether his mood had turned sour.

"So you might be interested to hear that one of Jennifer's neighbours, Denis Leclerc, goes past their house on his tractor every evening. Do you think it's possible that he might have tipped off the murderer to Adam's presence at the house that night?"

Yann frowned. Was he thinking about the investigation, or irritated by her questioning? But she had a sense that it would be wise to stop digging.

"So you have been talking to Jennifer," was all he said. It was a statement rather than a question. She looked at her watch and exclaimed, "Oh, look at the time. I didn't mean to stay so late."

He pushed his chair back without objection and escorted her to the front door where he gave her three kisses on the cheeks. She blushed.

"Three times, in Brittany," he said.

CHAPTER 27: AN ADMISSION

"Jonathan?"

He stirred beside Jennifer on the sofa, but said nothing and just picked up the TV remote to switch off. He petted Byron at their feet and waited for what she had to say. She knew he hated conversations about their relationship but she carried on anyway.

"Look, I need to know the truth about you and Emma . . ." she said. He interrupted her before she got into her stride.

"All right, all right. There's no need to keep banging on about it!" He glanced at her sideways before admitting, "Yes I did have a little fling but it's over now and honestly it was meaningless. It was when we were having to deal with all the stuff about Mariam."

Jennifer said nothing. She cast her mind back over the betrayals of the last few months, the known ones and the unknown.

"Oh, I see," she said eventually, her voice heavy with sarcasm. Jonathan was staring at her, waiting. "So Emma was your shoulder to cry on? And I had nobody while trying to hold our family together and support Mariam after that bullying led to some sort of existential crisis for her. I'm not sure that you even noticed our family was collapsing!"

Her repressed feelings came bubbling to the surface. "I'm the one putting in all the work on the smallholding as well as taking photos and doing the school run. But your main contribution is to check that Luke does his homework before he gets out his video game!"

"I do the school run too, I'll have you know. And I would remind you that I'm the one who pays the bills," he protested. He seemed taken aback by her outburst.

"Anyway, I just said I'm sorry, didn't I?" he insisted, his face close to hers. "I told you it's over!"

Jennifer backed away and stared back at him, her arms folded. How could she believe him? He'd lied to her for all this time.

"Ha!" she exclaimed. "That's a good one. The truth is that you've been gaslighting me since the beginning of the school term, making me feel that I'm worrying about nothing. And I believed your lies and excuses about Emma. Even Derek knew you were cheating on me. You humiliated me and you call it a little fling!"

Jonathan had recoiled into the comfort of the blue sofa cushions. He seemed to be considering his next move under her blistering gaze.

He reached across for her, in the first act of tenderness in months. She stiffened. It was going to take more than that to be forgiven.

"I'm sorry. I should have thought of you." He squeezed her arm. "But I swear, it's over."

The two of them sat facing the blank screen of the television for a moment while Jennifer considered whether to deliver an ultimatum. But she shrank back as her emotions welled up again. For the first time she wondered whether they both had the same interest in keeping their family together.

"I honestly feel that you should have been more engaged in helping Mariam get back on track. And I'm not just talking about helping her with maths," she said in a low voice. She'd remembered that the children were upstairs.

"What do you mean?"

"I mean why did you always leave everything to me? I was the one who rang the headmistress, and who comforted Mariam. And it was me who tracked down the child who was bullying her, and told her mother that it had better stop."

"You did what? Why didn't you tell me? Who is it? I thought you said the head had sorted it out ages ago." Now it was his voice being raised in anger.

"What difference does it make who it is? In fact the mother happens to be one of my customers, now an ex-customer, and so I actually shot myself in the foot out of love for my daughter."

Jennifer burst into tears at the memory of her encounter with Madame Seznec, prompting Jonathan to put his arm round her to comfort her. This time, she allowed it, and dropped her head onto his shoulder. She felt drained.

"We'll be OK, Jen, I promise," he said softly. "I'm sorry."

He took her face into his hands and his brown eyes locked on to hers.

He tried to kiss her on the cheek, but she pulled away. It was still too soon. She wiped away a tear with the back of her hand, and got up, stumbling over the prone figure of Byron.

"Oh get out of the way, you stupid dog!" she exclaimed. His head jerked up, his ears raised in surprise. He wasn't used to being treated like this.

Jennifer went into the kitchen where she put the kettle on. Jonathan followed her, with Byron swaying behind him in case a tasty morsel might be dropped.

"I agree that we should be showing Mariam a united front. Encourage her to bring friends over, that sort of thing. Luke is always hanging out with his," Jonathan said, attempting to guide the conversation back onto more neutral territory. He took out a couple of mugs from the cupboard and dropped a teabag into them.

"Yes, but he's perfectly integrated now. She has obviously felt treated like an outsider at school. I guess all we can do is talk to her and try to understand," said Jennifer.

She picked up the mugs and took them back into the living room where they returned to their places beside each other on the sofa.

"Truce?" he ventured.

She glanced across at him before nodding.

"And on Luke, by the way, what is it with that child?" Jonathan said. "Why does he refuse to speak English? Is he rejecting us or what?"

Jennifer shrugged. "I think it's a phase they go through. A peer group thing. I mean he's surrounded by French kids, and all his friends are French."

She picked up the TV remote and switched on the television. She started flicking through the channels before muting the sound.

"Jonathan?"

"Yes?" He sounded wary.

"Do you think we should invite Meredith over for Christmas?"

He didn't reply straight away.

"Why? Isn't Christmas a family affair? And it's not as though she's on her own. She's got Emma and Romy. And if we were inviting anyone it would have been my mother."

"That's true. It's just that I feel sorry for Meredith."

"Yeah. Awful." He picked up their mugs from the coffee table in front of them and headed for the kitchen. "Look, we'll have a great Christmas with the kids here on our own. And haven't we got some chickens to pluck?"

* * *

The next day, Jennifer caught Pippa's eye as she was packing up after the Christmas market, swollen by stalls of Breton trinkets and mulled wine. Business had been brisk, despite the cold, and she'd sold every last egg and chicken. She'd noticed Solenn selling her jewellery, while draped in her trademark designs, at the far end of the square.

Jennifer gestured in the direction of the café, and she and Pippa met up a few minutes later.

"*Un p'tit cognac?*" the waiter joked as they sat down at the back, divesting themselves of hats, scarves and jackets. He turned towards the bar where the locals had lined up their *ballons de rouge* on the zinc counter.

Jennifer ordered coffees as usual and waved. "There's Philippe and Jean-Luc, thick as thieves as usual," she said. "Shall we invite them over?"

"Why not?" By now Pippa had become friendly with the majority of the regular salespeople on the market, some of whom had become her customers.

Jennifer beckoned to the two men who came to stand by their table and held up their glasses to toast them a "Joyeux Noel".

They discussed the day's takings and it seemed that the four of them — selling cheese, pancakes, curry and chickens — were well pleased. After a few minutes of exchanging pleasantries about the weather, the two men returned to the bar when the waiter delivered their coffees.

"I wish it was Christmas every week, that was my best market ever," said Pippa. "I've been handing out flyers about the bakery opening soon. And I've found a sidekick. Now all I have to do is to finish my apprenticeship and pass my exams!"

"That's so exciting. I can't wait," said Jennifer. "When are you back?"

"In the New Year. You're staying here, aren't you?"

"Yes, it'll be just us. Jonathan had talked about inviting his mum but she's going to the Caribbean. All right for some, don't you think?"

"So that worked out well then . . ."

Jennifer smiled. She'd already told Pippa on the phone about Jonathan's confession. "It's not that I don't like her but . . . she invades. It's like she sucks up all the oxygen in the room, she never shuts up and leaves her stuff everywhere. I must say it crossed my mind that I should have told him to spend Christmas with her, but it's too late now. Even though he swears it's over, I'm not sure I can believe him."

"Maybe it's best to try and move on," said Pippa. "For the family's sake."

Jennifer wrinkled her nose. "Easier said than done. Although he does seem genuinely contrite."

Pippa finished her coffee and set it down. "Do you want a croissant? They're so good here, almost as good as mine."

Jennifer smiled and shook her head. "No, but thank you anyway. How are things going with your friendly neighbourhood gendarme?"

Pippa made a face. "I think I screwed up," she admitted. "Just when I thought things were hotting up. He invited me round to dinner at his place for the first time, and I think I overdid it by asking too much about the investigations."

"Really? Which ones?" Jennifer wanted to know. They both smiled.

"I thought I was helping Yann by mentioning the name of your farmer neighbour. But that made him realise I'd spoken to you about the murder suspect in Adam's case. I felt as though I'd betrayed his trust because he'd sworn me to secrecy."

"Ouch. I'm sorry."

"Yes. It was awkward. So I don't know where things stand between us now." She grimaced. "We'll see if the gendarmes follow it up. But he also told me that they know Craig wasn't killed by a rifle shot. It was a handgun apparently." She raised a finger to her lips. "And that's also top secret, by the way."

"Does it matter that it wasn't a rifle?"

"I suppose it does if they can narrow down the possible suspects. Although if they do find the murder weapon, they might not be able to prove who fired it. And Yann said it might be an illegal gun, in which case . . ." She raised her hands in the air.

"I presume they've interviewed everyone who was at the dress rehearsal," said Jennifer. "I mean, it was nearly three weeks ago now."

"But how would they know who else was there apart from all of us? The people who were standing at the back?"

"It gives me the shivers to think that the murderer is out there. I'm going to find out whether anyone else took pictures that night, apart from Meredith who did the video," Jennifer said, thinking aloud. "It would make sense, wouldn't it? I mean it was the dress rehearsal. I'll ask around."

"I saw Solenn taking pictures. Maybe others did too. But don't you think the police would have thought of that already?"

"Well, they certainly didn't ask me when they called, and I'm a photographer."

Pippa got up and gave Jennifer a high five. "OK, Madame Poirot, go for it!"

CHAPTER 28: CHRISTMAS

"Best Christmas ever," Luke announced from the floor. He was stretched out on the rug in the living room in front of a giant jigsaw puzzle.

"No it wasn't," said Mariam. Jennifer braced herself. What was she going to come out with now?

"We didn't have crackers," said Mariam, pulling a face. Jonathan winked at Jennifer and they relaxed.

"They don't do Christmas crackers in France as you know perfectly well," said Jennifer, mock sternly. "No carol service either. I miss that, actually. I used to know the descant to 'Hark the Herald'."

Luke sat up holding the last piece of the Tower of London and placed it triumphantly onto the puzzle. They all applauded.

"So now what do we do?" Mariam asked. Her voice was petulant.

"A walk, of course, before it gets dark," said Jennifer, and Luke went to pull on his wellies in the hall.

"I'm not coming," said Mariam. "I'm going to my room."

"Come on, Byron!" said Luke, ignoring Mariam.

The dog raised its muzzle before sinking to the stone floor again.

"I think that's a no," said Jennifer. "He's too tired."

She felt that at last she'd got her family back. They'd celebrated Christmas the French way on Christmas Eve. Jonathan had cracked open some oysters, she'd cooked a goose and they'd gorged on a Yuletide log. She and Jonathan had got drunk on champagne, and the children had stayed at the table without taking out their phones or surreptitiously handing down pieces of meat to the dog.

"I wonder how Meredith's Christmas went," said Jennifer. "Their first without Craig."

"Yes. Tough. But what do you want to do about it?"

"I was thinking of maybe having her over. Or what about inviting the Louennec players tomorrow? It will be Boxing Day, maybe they're at a loose end?"

"But what about their families? It's a family time, isn't it?"

"You keep saying that," she laughed. "But seriously, why not?"

"OK, let's get in touch with the usual suspects when we get back," he said.

They tramped along a path through the woods at the bottom of the garden. Luke ran ahead with a stick that he found on the ground. They always made sure he had one in case he slipped on the damp grass or came across a snake in the undergrowth.

They headed down to the stream in single file along the narrow path. The trees were bare and made a ghostly sound as the branches rustled in the breeze. The sky was darkening when they began to climb back up the slope towards the house.

As they approached the front gate, Jennifer could hear the cock crowing.

"Can you hear him? He's so annoying when he draws attention to himself like that, at any time of day or night."

Then she saw him, flapping his shiny black wings in the middle of the front garden. What was he doing there?

"Can you catch him?" Jennifer called out to Jonathan, pointing at the cock, and ran towards the wired chicken enclosure to see what had happened.

Luke had already run ahead, and called out, "Mummy!" with panic in his voice. "The gate to the chicken run is open!"

She almost tripped over a couple of russet *cous nus* scratching in the flowerbed in the dusk in their new-found freedom. She grabbed one of them, pinning its wings to its side to pick it up. It emitted a loud cluck of surprise. The other one made a dash for it and disappeared round the corner of the house.

"Shit!" she said out loud. Who had left the gate open? This had never happened before, even though it was only fastened with two bungee cords.

"Shut it!" she shouted to Luke as she arrived with the first hen. He was standing guard by the gate with his stick.

Jonathan followed her into the coop holding the cock.

"How many got out?" he asked her.

Jennifer dropped the hen onto the ground and made her way into the henhouse. She had to switch on her phone torch to see into the corners in the fading light in order to count. They kept a dozen laying hens plus the cock but she could only make out four of the grey *cendrées* inside.

Jonathan shoved the struggling cock into the henhouse and Jennifer shut the door behind them.

"Well?" he asked.

"There are four in there, plus the one I caught, plus the other *cou nu*, plus the cock…"

"So you mean that the six others have escaped? That's a great Christmas present for the fox!" he said.

"Damn," said Jennifer. "I'm going in to get Mariam. We'll have to get a search party out. They can't be far away."

She pushed open the front door and found Byron lying on his back with his paws in the air by the fire, a picture of creature comfort. He turned his head lazily towards her. A few years ago he would have leaped out of the house, she thought, but now the prospect of a chicken chase wouldn't even cause him to stir.

She raced upstairs and opened the door to the bedroom where Mariam was seated at her computer.

"What?" Mariam turned round, as though annoyed at the interruption.

"Somebody's let the hens out! We need you to help round them up. Come on, it's all hands on deck!" Jennifer insisted, waiting for Mariam to switch off and help.

Jonathan was waiting for them outside the front door with Luke.

"Right," he said. "Jennifer, you take the back garden, there's a chance the *cou nu* is still there, and maybe others. Mariam, you check the front."

"But what if I see one? Am I supposed to pick it up?"

"It's easy," said Jennifer. "Don't worry, they won't peck you." She demonstrated the best way to do so but still Mariam didn't seem convinced.

"Just call us if you find one," Jennifer conceded. "Let's get on with it."

"I'll go along to the fish pond," said Jonathan.

"I'm coming with you!" said Luke.

"No, you're going to stay by the entrance, so you can open the gate if we come back with a chicken. OK?"

"OK," they said in unison. They fanned out, screwing up their eyes in the fading light, in a fruitless search for six hens.

As they scoured every corner of the property, Jennifer had only one thought on her mind: who would have committed such an act of sabotage on Christmas Day? And why?

CHAPTER 29: CONNECTIONS

The guests trickled in bearing gifts the next evening.

Derek and Solenn arrived carrying a tray filled with their famous shrimp canapés which they insisted were leftovers. Meredith brought a bottle of champagne and apologised for Emma's absence, saying that she had to look after Romy.

Jennifer knew it was probably an excuse but was relieved. They had enough on their plate without the green-eyed monster.

She'd cut up slices of oven hot *boudin blanc* which they speared with cocktail sticks as they sat around the Christmas tree.

"It's so good to see you," she said to the little group. Pippa was away, and Mark had also sent regrets from England.

"We were wondering whether to go ahead with this because we had a Christmas disaster yesterday. Somebody let the chickens out and we've lost six good layers."

"How dreadful!" said Meredith. She leaned forward to spear a piece of sausage.

"Yes. Three Leghorns, and three Marans which lay those lovely copper- coloured eggs, are gone. The fox will have had a tasty Christmas dinner," Jennifer went on. "And the worst thing is that it was only in September when a weasel got into the henhouse and killed four chickens."

"Have you any idea who did it?" Derek asked.

"I was thinking that it might be something to do with us being English, maybe. You know they don't like outsiders here. I mean, Adam was targeted in our garden, wasn't he?" said Jennifer.

She sighed. Jonathan said, "Jennifer is only speculating, of course."

"I wonder if it might be connected with Craig?" said Meredith. "I wish I knew whether they're making any progress on Craig's murder. They've told me nothing."

"So, let's think about this," said Jennifer. "On the night of the dress rehearsal, Derek was at the front, but you and Solenn were sitting at the back with me, right?"

The two women nodded, wondering where this was going.

"And did you notice people who were standing behind you, near the hall entrance? I think I remember seeing some villagers in the dark. Had Craig let people know about the dress rehearsal?"

"I suppose he did," said Meredith. "He might have mentioned it to somebody on the council. And he had to book the hall, so it would have been common knowledge."

"There were people behind us, yes," said Solenn.

"OK. And were any of you taking pictures that night? Apart from Meredith, of course."

"I already sent the video to the police," said Meredith. "I must say I've not had time to watch it myself."

"I can show you what I have on my phone," said Solenn. "The police also have a copy." She got up and rummaged around in her leather handbag.

"Here we are," she said. " There's Mark. He was at the back too. But behind it was dark. Look here."

She handed her phone to Jennifer. She could make out two figures in the doorway, behind the rows of chairs, but the faces were in the shadows. She pinched the screen to enlarge the photos but could see nothing but an unfocused shape.

"Oh well," Jennifer said. "It was worth a try."

Jonathan shot her a hostile look as though to say, why even mention it then? Then he held up a hand. "Look everyone. It's Christmas. So let's talk about something else. Such as what did you all have for Christmas dinner?"

He turned to Solenn. "Do you ever talk about anything other than food? What about the weather?"

Solenn smiled. "But have you noticed what we do? When we are having a meal, we always talk about one that we've had earlier, not the one we're eating."

The conversation drifted back to Craig and how he was missed. Meredith reminisced about his last job in Bridgwater. "The worst thing that happened to him was when he sent the wrong page to be printed. On his paper, they put dummy copy onto the page and it was his job to check. But one night he never noticed until it was too late that it had gone out with 'seasons of mellow fruitfulness' instead of a news article!"

"He might have got away with it if it had been a review of *The Cherry Orchard*," Jonathan remarked.

Meredith ignored him and shook her head. "He was mortified. He cared a lot about his job. I know people thought he was bossy but, in fact, he was a very caring person. That's why he got elected onto the council here. He wanted to make people's lives better."

"Yes. That was his legacy," said Derek. Everyone nodded. There was no point in remembering what a pain in the neck he'd been.

"Didn't the priest mention at the funeral that he'd worked in London as a business reporter?" Jonathan asked. "I knew quite a few of them when we lived there."

"Oh yes, but that was years ago," said Meredith. "He lost his job, and that's when we decided to leave London and move to Somerset. And we stayed there until we came here."

Almost as though talking to herself, she continued, "But do you know what hurt me the most? That his passing was so

... so *unseemly*. I mean, to die in the middle of a pantomime, dressed in breeches and that stupid hat ... " She looked for her handbag and took out a hanky to wipe away a tear.

"Have you thought about running for the council yourself?" Jennifer asked her gently. "Don't you think it would be a good idea to continue his work?"

Meredith's dark eyes were hooded. "To be honest I haven't really thought about it seriously because his seat is going to be left vacant till the next elections anyway."

"Yes, but aren't they scheduled in a few months?"

"Emma doesn't think I should run. It's a lot of work, you know. I'm not sure I've got the energy. And secondly, although most of the councillors are independents, Craig was always complaining about how difficult it was to reach agreement on anything. He was particularly critical of Mathieu, he said he was a hypocrite and so on."

"What about Craig's work opposing the wind turbines in Louennec? You can't just drop it now," said Jonathan. "Jennifer's always taking photos of some farmer or other who's agreed a contract with the developers. If we're not careful, the village will be overrun by the damned things."

"Why don't you run, then?" Meredith said, sharply.

Jonathan retorted: "Because I'm not French."

There was an awkward silence. It was the first time it had crossed Jennifer's mind that Meredith might not like Jonathan. Could it be to do with Emma?

Jonathan got up in search of another bottle of wine from the kitchen.

"We're on visas and permits, like everyone else who got here after Brexit," Jennifer explained. "We won't be able to vote for you, I'm afraid. All that's changed."

"We both got citizenship about five years ago," said Meredith. "You have to live here for five consecutive years before you can apply. But Craig was already on the council before then."

"Lucky you," said Jennifer. "But we'll get there ... So tell us, what brought you two to France in the first place?"

Meredith accepted a top-up from Jonathan before replying. "Craig got redundancy from his paper in Bridgwater, and I realised that I could teach English here, so we decided to take the plunge. The surprise was when Emma decided to join us with Romy shortly afterwards. She'd just divorced, you see, and wanted a change. We put some money into her kitchen store, to help her settle here. I guess like so many of us, she wanted to do something completely different."

"Romy seems well integrated," said Jonathan. "Was that a challenge at first?"

"Of course. She was the only English kid in her class, and I think the others thought she was weird. But she soon picked up French."

"And does Romy talk to you in French?" Jonathan asked.

"Oh yes," said Meredith. "And I reply in English. It's not a big deal."

Jonathan winked at Jennifer. So Luke wasn't the only one.

Jennifer was still thinking about Craig. She looked around the room, examining her friends as though they were potential accomplices. Had someone on the stage given a signal to the shooter? But the only people there had been Jonathan, Pippa and Craig himself. Derek had been sitting at the piano near the stage. What might he have seen? And what about Solenn?

Then, almost as an afterthought, she said to Meredith: "Could you let me have a copy of your video from the dress rehearsal? I'd love to see that."

CHAPTER 30: PIPPA

It was at times like this that Pippa wished she smoked, like the other candidates waiting outside the anonymous building in Rennes where they were to take their final exam.

They all seemed to be in their twenties, if not younger, and had gravitated towards each other on the pavement, where they were now chatting animatedly and puffing on their vapes or cigarettes. She overheard them gossiping about the first exam which had tested their knowledge of food safety, hygiene and management issues.

That test had lasted ninety minutes, but now they were waiting for the real exam, seven hours of baking. Pippa just wanted to get the practical over with, but was still nervous.

She filed in behind the others, her throat dry. Not for the first time she asked herself, *Why am I doing this?*

The baker in the *boulangerie* where she'd completed her apprenticeship in January had predicted that Pippa would pass with flying colours. She'd got on much better with Rozenn, a middle-aged mother hen who ran a bakery in a village outside Carhaix, than with Loic.

"You'll see, you won't even have to think about what you're baking," Rozenn had said. "You could do it blindfold."

But Pippa couldn't help worrying that she'd burn the baguettes, or forget an ingredient in the dough.

Seven hours later, she emerged exhausted but happy, having baked the full range of bread and *viennoiseries* that she'd soon be selling in her own bakery. Everything from baguettes, pain de campagne and brioche, to croissants, pains au chocolat and pains aux raisins, had gone well. Rozenn had been right.

Pippa followed the other candidates out of the building. She was still high on adrenalin and felt like calling after them in case they wanted to relax over a glass of wine in a nearby café. But they turned a corner and disappeared without saying goodbye.

She drove back to Louennec. As she turned into her street, she noticed Mark going into the bar-tabac and remembered that she hadn't said anything to the owners about her plans to open the bakery only a few yards away from their café. In fact, despite living in the village for months, she'd still never gone inside. She'd always thought it would be a gloomy bar full of men like Mark, drinking themselves under the table after placing bets.

She parked in her drive and walked straight over. She pushed open the door into a brightly lit room where the shelves behind the till were stocked with cigarettes and sweets. A man was buying stamps from the owner. Pippa realised this must be Michel, a stout man in his early forties with a ruddy complexion from either an outdoor life or a surfeit of alcohol. Behind him was a rack containing a couple of baguettes. There was also a newspaper stand near the entrance with a few remaining copies of the day's local papers.

"*Bonjour*," Pippa murmured, and looked around. The little café was furnished with a few small tables covered in red-and-white chequered tablecloths. She saw Mark sinking a glass of draught beer at the far end of the bar.

"Mind if I join you?" she asked, sidling up to him.

"Be my guest. What brings you here?"

"I feel like celebrating. I've just finished my bakery exams and unless I made a catastrophic mistake like King Alfred, I'll be able to go ahead with my grand opening!"

"That's great." Mark smiled. "So, what's your poison?"

"Ooh, maybe I'll push the boat out and have a Muscadet," she said with a smile. "The sun's gone down over the yardarm, hasn't it?"

"There's always somewhere in the world, I find."

Mark called Michel over to order, but before he could, Pippa introduced herself to him and said with her most disarming smile, "I don't know if you've heard, but I'm the competition. I'm opening a bakery along the street here. I'm sorry, I should have told you before . . ."

Michel burst out laughing. "So you are Peeper? We were wondering when you'd tell us," he said. She should have known.

Mark winked at her and ordered her wine. "News travels fast in this place," he said.

"It's a shame about the panto, isn't it?" she said. It was the first subject of conversation that she could think of. "I mean, a shame about Craig too, of course."

Mark stared into his beer before replying. "I can't say that panto's my thing, actually."

Pippa tried not to laugh. "Yes, the rest of us had noticed that."

Michel returned with her Muscadet. "I hear you're taking on Gwen, Daniel's daughter, at the bakery?"

So that was how he knew. Her future apprentice was the nineteen-year-old daughter of a local farmer, who was doing a bakery course and living with her parents in the village.

"Ah, and so is Daniel a customer of yours?" Pippa asked.

He nodded. "Of course."

"That's good," said Pippa. "I hear that Gwen isn't afraid of hard work."

"She'll do well," said Michel. "Excuse me," he added, returning to the till where a customer wanted to buy a lottery ticket.

"I don't think they're worried about the competition from you, frankly," Mark commented.

"It doesn't seem so, does it? I was getting quite anxious about it."

"So, tell me about the grand opening." It was the first time he'd ever asked her a direct question. Maybe he was just shy.

"You're all invited, of course," said Pippa. "I'm doing a few special bakes for the opening. I'm really excited about it, now that everything's been installed."

"But what gave you the idea to open a bakery here?"

Pippa took a long sip of wine before responding. "Why are any of us here?" she said. "I'd taken a payoff from my job in finance and I wanted to do something completely different. What about you? Why did you move here? I mean, you're an accountant, aren't you?"

Mark stared at the glasses behind the bar before replying, so much so that she began to wonder whether he'd heard her question. Eventually, without making eye contact with her, he said, "Well, it's a long story. And I'm going to be moving back to England. That's what I was organising over Christmas. But the reason I decided to move from London in the first place was because my wife died."

"Oh, oh dear, I'm so sorry," she said. "Was she sick?"

"She died by suicide,," said Mark, looking straight at her with a mournful gaze.

Pippa gripped his arm. "I'm sorry," she said. She studied his face, noticing for the first time the deep lines etched on his forehead.

"Thanks," he said. "It was a long time ago."

He raised his hand to catch Michel's attention. "Do you want another one?"

"Oh, thank you, but no, I'd better go home," she said. Mark's disclosure had made her feel awkward. She felt it wasn't appropriate to probe further when they hardly knew each other. "Got a lot of stuff to do. See you at the opening, then."

CHAPTER 31: THE VIDEO

Jennifer could hear Jonathan chopping wood when she left the house to pick up the children. He stopped when he saw the car drive past, wiped his brow and waved.

She hated January. Not only were the days so short, but it seemed to rain constantly. The damp penetrated the house which struggled to heat through because of the draughty doors and windows. The crops they were harvesting were the cabbages that Luke disliked, as well as potatoes and leeks which found their way into warming soups. All organic, of course. It had taken them ages to obtain the certificates of approval so they could sell them at the market.

Then there were the sheep. Both the ewes were pregnant and would soon deliver. Things seemed to be working out, at last. Jonathan had thrown himself into their market garden with renewed vigour, and the children seemed to be thriving. They were both getting good marks at school. So why did she still feel unsettled?

She wondered what she'd be doing if they'd stayed in London. Maybe a fashion shoot with a model friend who sent work her way. Or a wedding. Her freelance jobs in London had an infinite variety, despite the lack of guaranteed income — something which had always been provided by Jonathan.

Compared to Louennec, her previous life seemed glamorous. But what was the point of comparing the two?

She'd spent the morning traipsing in her wellies through a field of winter wheat with a reporter and a farmer who was complaining about badger setts on his land. The paper was doing a story about damage by the badgers to his farm machinery. She took pictures of him standing by a hole which he said was a den containing a dozen badgers. But as soon as he felt the camera on him, he tensed. That was often the way, and she had to coax her subjects into relaxing. She already knew that she'd have to go out again the next day, on a story about the bad weather. The French farmers were always cursing about too much rain or too much sun. If they didn't get compensation, they'd dump piles of muck in town squares or send tractors down the motorway blocking traffic. That's how the farm lobby works here, she thought, despite getting the biggest EU subsidies.

She glanced at her hands on the steering wheel, the nails stained with grime and neglect. How long had it been since she'd had a manicure? And what about her hair? She noticed in the rear-view mirror that the grey was creeping along the roots. Was this what Jonathan saw when he looked at her? she wondered. When she thought of him, she still saw the dashing youth whom she'd met at school.

She was just thinking that she needed to book a hair appointment when she was jolted out of her reverie by Luke waving at her from the pavement outside his school. They headed to Carhaix to find Mariam, with Luke babbling in a mixture of French and English all the way. Mariam was waiting outside the school with Pervenche, who waved and walked off when they arrived.

Back home, she fell into the sofa with a sigh. Byron sat at her feet in front of the crackling fire which Jonathan had laid. After a moment, she got up to take advantage of the brief respite before dinner and fetched her laptop. She was scrolling through her old emails when she came across the file that Meredith had sent her after Christmas. She'd completely forgotten about it. She began playing the video whose images were sometimes jumpy when Meredith had put down the phone to perform her own lines as Fairy Nuff and the phone showed images of the ceiling. Jennifer hit the fast forward button to reach the final five minutes, about eighty minutes into the dress rehearsal.

There was Pippa flapping her arms and quacking, which made her laugh. Craig as the Demon King was sinister, pulling on the cord that bound her to him. Jonathan, as Mother Goose, seemed vulnerable compared to Craig. Meredith had zoomed in on Craig's facial expression, distorted with hatred as he faced the audience defiantly, telling them to "shut up, you lot!" He didn't turn round when Jonathan went to the back of the stage to pick up the rifle. He only did so when somebody called out "he's behind you" and the fatal shot rang out. But what Jennifer noticed was that a split second before that, Craig had caught sight of someone standing outside the hall, right at the back. And on his face was a look of recognition.

CHAPTER 32: THE GRAND OPENING

Pippa stroked the smooth surface of the stainless-steel counter with pride.

She'd put on a spotless white apron over a white T-shirt and tied her hair back with a scarf for the grand opening.

She'd stacked the bread on racks behind her, and neat piles of *viennoiseries* in the display counter. As she was putting the finishing touches, she received two phone messages. One was from her bakery course tutor wishing her good luck, and the second was from Yann.

It was 8 a.m. She took a deep breath, marched to the front of the bakery, raised the blinds and turned the sign on the door to OUVERT. Another in the window, draped with coloured paper decorations for the occasion, announced *Artisan Boulanger*. The workmen had revealed the original stonework on the inside walls which contrasted with the shiny new units.

Pippa opened the door. She was astonished to see Jennifer at the head of a small queue, holding three balloons. She stepped in, saying, "Congratulations, I wanted to be your first customer."

They hugged. Jennifer hooked the balloons on the door latch.

"Thank you," said Pippa. "What can I get you?"

"A *tradition*," said Jennifer. "*Pas trop cuite.*"

Pippa turned back to pick out a slightly undercooked baguette.

"By the way, how do you get the bread to cater for different tastes? Does your oven have shelves at different temperatures? I've always wondered."

Pippa noticed that the bakery had suddenly filled with people examining what she had on sale. She'd decided to make some sausage rolls, which she labelled *friands à la saucisse*, knowing that the Breton farmers liked food that would keep them going in the fields. In the cake department, rather than attempt to compete with the typical buttery Breton pastries such as Kouign amann and the Far breton, she'd baked cupcakes and a dozen festive *Tropézienne* cakes. She also displayed the French staples like her apple tarts. It was an Ali Baba cave of sweet delights.

She answered Jennifer's question. "Er, well, I'm going to let you into a secret," she said in a low voice. "The oven doesn't heat at an even temperature, so I get to know where the baguettes are *bien cuites*, and where they're not so *cuites*. Simple, really."

"Ah!" said Jennifer.

A woman in the queue was pressing behind her and clearing her throat with impatience.

"I'll get out of your way. Good luck," Jennifer added, getting out the coins to pay for her baguette before heading off.

"*Oui, Madame? Bonjour et bienvenue,*" Pippa said, smiling at the next customer.

She overheard another villager saying, "This is wonderful," as she smelled the freshly baked bread. She went off with some sausage rolls, saying to a friend, "It's so English!" Pippa wondered whether they might have donated to her fundraising. Another told her at the till that "it was time we had a proper bakery in Louennec". Another asked her where she was from and how come she spoke such good French.

She recognised some of the customers from her market stall. What she hadn't anticipated was that the *Tropéziennes*, made of fluffy brioche filled with a light cream and topped with crystallised sugar, would fly off the shelves.

Gwen arrived an hour later to prep the next batches for the afternoon in the back. Lunchtime brought another mini-rush. By late afternoon, when she'd invited her British friends to join her in a glass of fizz, she was exhausted. She knew that before she closed at 7.30 p.m. she'd have to make sure that Gwen had prepared the next day's dough.

Jennifer was again first to arrive, having collected the children from school. Pippa let them choose cakes to take home for free.

"How do you feel?" Jennifer asked. "It's obviously going really well!"

"I'm like a hamster on a treadmill. Thank goodness Gwen is here to help." Pippa pointed towards the back room where her apprentice was hard at work.

Mark came along and picked out a baguette before shaking Pippa's hand and helping himself to champagne behind the counter. Derek and Solenn followed him in and she took out a *Tropézienne* that she'd set aside for them.

"Oh, this makes a change," said Solenn. "I can't wait to try it!"

"They're straight from St Tropez," Pippa joked. "I thought, let's put a bit of sunshine into our lives."

And finally, Meredith, who chose some croissants and a pain au chocolat for the next morning. "This one's for Romy," she said.

At 5 p.m., Gwen brought in another batch of freshly baked bread from the back, and Pippa introduced her to her guests.

"Are you sure you want to do this job?" Meredith asked Gwen. "You know that bakers don't have a life."

"Ah but I'm used to getting up early," she replied, with a laugh. "My dad's a farmer. And I want to be my own boss."

The guests began trickling out, after wishing Pippa well. She was just about to close up and call her daughters to tell them about her first day when a white-haired woman came in. She was wearing a long mac and dark tights. There was nothing unusual about her except for the black eye that glistened above her left cheek. Pippa knew immediately who she was. She also noticed that she was limping.

"*Ça va, Madame?*" she asked from behind the till. It wasn't just a greeting but an expression of concern.

"*Oui, parfaitement,*" came the abrupt reply. The woman took her change from the state-of-the-art automated till in front of her and pushed past a young woman who was coming in with a child. She seemed to recognise the old lady and turned to watch her cross the road before muttering something under her breath.

"Am I too late?" she asked Pippa.

"It depends what you need."

The woman pointed to the remaining two baguettes and ordered one. She asked her daughter if she wanted a cake and the girl scrutinised the display.

"You know the lady who was just in here, do you?" Pippa asked in a low voice.

"Do I know her? Of course I do. She's the stepmother of the thugs who killed my husband!"

CHAPTER 33: A CLUE

The woman's daughter piped up, "I want an apple turnover."

"All right, *ma puce*. How much do I owe you, Madame?"

She paid and told the girl to wait outside with her pastry. Then she said to Pippa, "I am Didier's wife, Nathalie."

It suddenly all made sense.

"I'm so sorry. I didn't know your husband personally, but I knew about his efforts to try and stop the wind farm project. And you suspect the old lady's sons of pushing him into the slurry tank?"

Nathalie, a willowy blonde, nodded vigorously. "I found out that he'd been threatened by them before he died. I was too scared to challenge them, or to report them to the *gendarmerie*, but I went to the house and told Madame Briand that she should hand them in."

"Ah," said Pippa. "She must have said something to them and they responded by beating her up!"

"So you can see why I didn't report them. They would have come looking for me next!"

"But surely they weren't acting by themselves," said Pippa.

"It seems obvious to me that the wind farm developers must have been behind it, don't you think? I mean they're planning to build those three turbines on the other side of our fence, and Didier was leading the campaign to stop it!"

"I agree with you, it seems pretty clear to me too." Pippa had a thought. "Give me your name and phone number, and I'll do what I can."

She went into the back room where she took out her bakery notebook from a drawer and tore out a page.

"Don't worry, I'll be discreet," Pippa reassured her. After a moment's hesitation, Nathalie scribbled down her details and handed back the piece of paper, before picking up her baguette and turning to go. Her daughter was waiting outside on the pavement staring at them through the windowpane, munching on her turnover.

CHAPTER 34: A PLATE OF MUSSELS

Pippa was prowling round her kitchen a few days later after work, tidying up while thinking up a plan.

Her relations with Yann had been nothing other than cordial since Christmas. So that meant it was her turn to invite him to dinner, didn't it? But what would she do if she was rejected? She sighed.

She examined the contents of the fridge. She had some fresh mussels — enough for two — which had to be eaten that night. The advantage was that they were quick to cook, as long as she cleaned them properly. She rinsed them thoroughly under the cold tap, with one ear listening for the sound of a car door slamming.

At the very moment she heard Yann's car pulling into the drive, she opened the front door and took out some old newspapers which she dropped in the recycling bin.

"*Bonsoir*," she called out, with a wave. He locked the car and walked to the hedge.

"*Bonsoir*, Peeper. I was thinking about you," he said. "I have something of interest for you."

This was going better than expected.

"Really? Well, it so happens that I'm making *moules marinières* tonight, and I've got more than enough for one, if you want to come round later? I mean, if you're not too busy," she said, suddenly embarrassed.

"With great pleasure," he said with a grin.

"Say in about half an hour then?"

* * *

Pippa waited anxiously for the doorbell to ring. She'd prepared the sauce on the hob and had the mussels ready to drop in when Yann arrived. What news could he possibly have of interest? Maybe they'd found Craig's killer and she'd be the first to know.

The bell rang at last and she hurried to open it. Yann was standing outside holding up a baguette. "*Pas trop cuite*? It's one of yours, of course."

"*Pas trop cuite*," she nodded, taking the bread with a smile.

She took him into the kitchen, where the table was already set, and took out a chilled bottle of Gros Plant from the fridge. Yann offered to open it while she took care of the molluscs.

"What's this news then?" she asked, unable to restrain her curiosity.

"Ah," he said. He served them both a glass and drew up a chair. "Make sure you buy the paper, tomorrow," he added, refusing to say anything more. This was so unfair.

She served the steaming mussels in Breton pottery dishes, their distinctive iodine smell wafting from the pot. "Les moules de bouchot, the last of the season," she announced.

"Delicious. How are you?" he asked. "You always seem to be working. You must be tired."

"Shattered. Thank God I've got Gwen. She's brilliant."

"I hear on the grapevine it's going well. You've got a lot of happy customers. Congratulations." Yann held up his glass and they clinked.

"It's the hours. I should have realised it meant getting up at four every morning to do my first batch. And I can't do my market stall anymore because the bakery's open on Saturdays."

"What about Sundays?"

She laughed. "Yes. But only till lunchtime. I'm taking Mondays off. Or at least part of Monday because I'll have to prep for Tuesday. Do I sound like a workaholic?" — she searched for the word in French before remembering *un bourreau de travail*.

He smiled. "Don't worry, people can still go to the bar-tabac to pick up their bread when you're closed. I wonder how Michel and Solange feel about the competition from *une Anglaise*." The idea seemed to amuse him.

"Michel already knew when I told him about it. And Solange introduced herself when she came in to buy a cake the other day, so I think they're cool with it."

"Don't worry, I'm sure it's not a big deal for them," said Yann. "They've got the Loto and must be making a small fortune from selling vapes these days. So are you doing all right financially?"

He threw a mussel shell into a large plastic dish that Pippa had set down for the purpose. "These are delicious, by the way, they're so tender and creamy," he added. He wiped his hands on a paper napkin after mopping up the sauce with a torn piece of baguette.

"It's probably too early to tell," she responded. "But I've got my first catering order! Do you know the woman who lives in the house opposite here with blue shutters?"

"The one who leaves the children's toys outside? One of these days they're going to get stolen."

"But luckily a gendarme lives just across the street . . . Anyway, she wants a birthday cake for her nine-year-old daughter."

"Wonderful! But . . . when are we next going to see each other?"

She hadn't expected this and didn't answer. She stood up to dispose of the mussel shells.

"I'll do it," he said, getting up. They were suddenly standing next to each other. He put down the mussel shells on the counter and his arms enfolded her. She held her hands in the air, sticky from the sauce. She laughed nervously before he kissed her on the lips. She kissed him back. Then he picked up the mussel shells' dish and threw the contents in the kitchen bin as though nothing had happened.

"Coffee?" she asked, as though she needed more caffeine after that embrace.

"Of course." He smiled.

Pippa busied herself at the counter. *Did that really happen?*

She said over her shoulder, "Do you know who came in today? The woman I told you about who lives in the white house with her two stepsons."

"*Et alors?*"

"It so happens that she has a black eye. And she's limping."

He emitted a "pff". By now, she knew how to interpret it.

"I'm just saying that she's in danger."

"Did you say anything to her?"

"I asked her whether she was OK. She replied that she was perfectly fine."

"This is what I said to you. How can you help somebody who doesn't want to be helped?"

"OK. But something else happened today which puts a different light on the situation."

His demeanour changed so slightly that she knew she'd attracted his professional interest. She poured their coffees into espresso cups and sat down beside him at the kitchen table.

"Do you know the widow of Didier, who drowned in the slurry tank?"

"Nathalie. Yes, of course." He nodded curtly and drained his cup in one slurp. "We questioned her in connection with her husband's death."

"Well, she told me today that she'd heard that the old lady's sons were the ones who pushed him. And that she'd gone round to tell her to hand them in."

Yann frowned slightly and his head moved from side to side as though he was sifting evidence.

"And so you are suggesting that this is why Madame Briand has been injured?"

"What do you think?"

He continued to move his head. "Maybe, maybe not."

She wished he'd stop saying that. It must be something they learned in their training, she supposed.

"And Nathalie says that she's heard that it's the wind farm developers who were behind it."

Nothing betrayed Pippa's little white lie. Yann's brown eyes locked on to hers.

"Who did she hear this from?"

"She didn't say . . ."

"I see. Leave this with me, Peeper. Promise me that you will not get involved. I will take it from here. OK?"

He took her hand and squeezed it, before raising her fingers to his lips.

"OK, I promise," she replied.

He got up and they hugged again. This time their kiss was long and languorous. She wondered whether to invite him into her bed, but as she hesitated, he was already turning to leave.

"And don't forget to buy the paper," he said.

CHAPTER 35: A BREAKTHROUGH

Jennifer heard a loud bellow from outside and sat up bolt upright in bed. She hadn't heard Jonathan get up and realised that it was his voice calling her name.

"Coming!" she shouted. She grabbed her dressing gown and ran downstairs. The house filled with noise. She heard the children scrambling out of bed.

Jonathan ran inside. "Call the vet!"

"What on earth's happened?"

"It's the sheep. It looks like Rambo has head-butted the youngster, who's lying on the ground, but something's also happened to one of the ewes. She's lost her lamb."

"Oh no!"

Jennifer picked up her phone. Luckily their vet was on Sunday duty and promised to be there within the hour.

"Marie-Laure's coming," she said. "Let me see the ewe."

As she was putting on her wellies she heard a stampede down the wooden staircase. Luke was the first to arrive, followed by Mariam and Pervenche who'd stayed for a sleepover.

"You stay here," Jennifer said to them. "Mariam, can you make breakfast for the three of you?"

"Can't we come too?" said Mariam.

"No," said Jonathan. "Your mother and I are taking care of this."

The three of them looked at each other before drifting away to the kitchen where Mariam put the kettle on. Jennifer followed Jonathan to the pasture, but she was halfway there before she realised it was raining. She gasped when he opened the gate. The ewe had collapsed onto the ground next to a puddle of yellow and red liquid where her dead lamb lay.

"Oh the poor thing," she said, running forward. She was drenched but hardly noticed. They heard a vehicle approaching and Jonathan went to greet Marie-Laure. She was a slight young woman in a hooded mac and carried a bag laden with surgical equipment. Her frame seemed too small for the strenuous tasks at hand. She knelt down to examine the ewe. The vet's arm disappeared inside the animal.

"She'll survive," she said, getting up. "She was only carrying one lamb. This is her first?"

"Yes," said Jennifer. "But there's another who's pregnant. She must be in the shelter."

"I'll check her out," said the vet. "But what's happened here?"

She'd noticed the young ram lying on its side in the pasture, its head bloodied, and went over.

"I think it was head-butted by the old ram," said Jonathan.

"He gave it a hell of a bash." She felt the animal before looking up at them. "He's gone, I'm afraid."

Jennifer burst into tears. Jonathan came over to comfort her.

"Where's the other ewe?"

"In here." Jonathan led the way into the shelter where Rambo stood in a dark corner. A sheep stood in the other corner, as though trying to keep as far as possible from the patriarch.

"So he's the culprit," said the vet, shaking her head. "They do that when they want to assert themselves. But not usually so violently."

Marie-Laure walked through the hay to the pregnant ewe who kicked up her feet while being examined. But the vet held her tightly.

"She'll be ready in a couple of weeks," she said. "Let me know if you need any help."

She tore off a piece of paper from a notebook in her mac pocket and wrote down a phone number before handing it to Jonathan. "You'll need this specialised company to dispose of the other one and the dead lamb."

"What's that?" Jennifer asked Jonathan.

"I presume it's a knacker's yard," he said quietly. "Thank you, *docteur*... er, Madame."

They escorted her back to her van, their clothes dripping in the rain. Jonathan gripped Jennifer by the shoulders. She was still crying, and shivering in the cold.

They waved to the vet as she drove away along the muddy drive. "I didn't know what to call her," he said with a wry grin.

"She looked so young, I almost called her *tu*," said Jennifer. They both still got tied in knots over the intricacies of when to address a person by the more familiar *tu* form rather than the more formal *vous*. It was particularly stressful when the person concerned switched from one to the other in the same conversation, if not the same sentence.

"You need to get inside," Jonathan said.

"They're only dead sheep, for God's sake. Why am I so upset?" Jennifer was laughing at herself, but couldn't stop the sobs.

"It's our everyday story of country folk."

They walked back along the track towards the house. Jennifer took out her phone and discovered that she had a voicemail message from Pippa as well as texts from her and Meredith, both instructing her to read the morning paper.

"I'll catch you up," she said to Jonathan. "I'll see if the paper's been delivered."

She snatched the morning's *Le Télégramme* from the letterbox by the front gate. The pages had stuck together in the damp. The front page had a bullet announcement about Adam's murder and she turned to the Louennec page for the full story where she read that two men had been arrested. She scanned the article quickly. It explained that the English estate agent had been blackmailed by a villager who was threatening to kill him. He wanted regular payments in compensation for allegedly paying over the odds for a house which turned out to have serious problems. Adam was killed after failing to make a payment. She noticed though that the article seemed to be quite sympathetic to the villager who had been placed under investigation for murder, pointing out that locals were being priced out of the housing market by the influx of expats. The second man was accused of assisting the murderer. Jennifer knew exactly who it was.

She ran into the house. Jonathan was making tea in the kitchen.

"They've got Adam's murderer!" she shouted. "And it's obviously because they followed up what we said about Denis Leclerc tipping off the murderer on our party night."

"That's brilliant," he said, seizing the paper. "Let me look."

Jennifer rang Pippa. "We did it!"

"Yes, and for once, we've been thanked by a grateful gendarme," said Pippa. "Champers all round!"

CHAPTER 36: BITTER APPLES

That same evening, as the family was finishing dinner, Meredith rang to ask if she could come over.

"I hope she's all right," said Jennifer. *Haven't we had enough drama for one day?* she thought to herself.

The children were upstairs and presumed to be doing their homework when the doorbell rang. Byron gave a half-hearted bark from his blanket on the floor before sinking down again.

They hung up Meredith's heavy waterproof cape, Jonathan made coffee, and the three of them sat round the kitchen table. It seemed like a formal meeting, as Meredith rarely called on them without a reason.

"First of all, I wanted to make sure you'd seen the paper. Isn't it wonderful? They've arrested Adam's murderer at last," said Meredith. "The poor guy was being blackmailed. Who'd have guessed?"

Jennifer and Jonathan exchanged smiles of satisfaction. "Yes, it's great news," said Jennifer. "But what's up?"

"There's something I wanted to mention," Meredith went on. "I've decided to run in the council elections."

"Is this to do with honouring Craig's memory?" Jennifer asked.

"Yes and no," Meredith replied. "Something happened to one of my neighbours which is what prompted my decision."

She explained how the council had changed the zoning classification of a plot of land belonging to her neighbours from constructible to non-constructible.

"Except that nobody from the council informed the family concerned, and so when they decided to sell the apple orchard last month in order to build a house, they discovered it was non-constructible! What sort of council does a thing like that? It's funny that Craig never mentioned it to me," she grumbled. "Apparently there was a vote in the council three months ago when they reviewed the zoning. My neighbours had two months to contest the decision but as they weren't even aware of it . . . and I can tell you there's a big difference in terms of what the land is worth now . . . I mean, honestly!" she went on.

"From what you're saying, it's too late to help them if you're elected," Jonathan said.

"Yes, of course, but it's the principle, isn't it? You can't behave like that if you're the member of an elected body serving your community!" Meredith took a sip of her espresso. "We need more transparency, obviously."

She lowered her voice. "Between you and me, I think that's the way Mathieu likes to run things. Look at the way he handled the wind turbines, I think we don't know the half of it."

"Really?" said Jennifer. "I think you should definitely run. I'm sure you can make a difference."

Meredith stretched across the table and patted her on the hand. "Thank you, dear. I wanted to know if I would have your support. Because I'm going to have to campaign, aren't I?"

"Are you going to run as an independent? And have you got the energy? It's a lot of work," Jonathan pointed out.

"Are you saying I'm too old?"

"No, no!" he protested.

"I will run as an independent, most of the councillors do that. I can only think of one or two who are aligned with a political party, and they're ecologists," she said. "I mean the issues we deal with are basically local, so that's why they're not necessarily politically affiliated."

"But I thought Mathieu was a member of Les Républicains?" said Jennifer. "He's right-wing, isn't he?"

"I'm sure he is. But he never mentions it," said Meredith.

"If you need any flyers making up, or delivering, let me know," Jennifer volunteered.

"That's sweet of you. Thank you." Meredith got up awkwardly. "Ouch, It's the gout. Incredibly painful."

"Again? Have you been hitting the bottle?"

"I'd have plenty reasons to, wouldn't I? But basically, it's a build-up of crystals in the toes. I've got pills for when it flares up. Sometimes it hurts to have even the weight of a sheet on my leg at night."

"Are you doing OK, Meredith? I mean, you must miss Craig terribly," said Jennifer.

Meredith's eyes dampened before she replied. "I think that's why I need to run for the council. It will give me something useful to do instead of just clearing up his affairs in that big old house."

"And what about the investigation?" Jonathan asked. "Have you heard anything?"

"Not a thing," she said, shaking her head.

Jennifer remembered something. "Meredith, you know the video you sent me? The one of the dress rehearsal? I think you should raise it with the police."

"Why's that? They've got it already."

"Take a look yourself, right at the end. I'm convinced that Craig knew the killer." Jennifer explained what she'd seen in the final frames.

"Oh my goodness," she said. "I'll certainly do that."

She went into the hall to pick up her cape. "I've got to get my skates on now. The election campaign starts in the middle of March, so there's not much time to get organised!" she said to Jennifer who opened the door to see whether it was still raining. A damp mist had descended with the darkness.

"I don't know why you offered to help her. Do you think she's got a hope in hell of being elected? I mean Craig wasn't exactly flavour of the month, was he?" Jonathan said, after Meredith had gone.

"Frankly, I admire her for doing it. Her heart's in the right place and I think that we should stick together. Because we Brits are all in the same boat, aren't we?"

CHAPTER 37: AN ALLY

It was a quiet afternoon at the bakery.

Pippa was in the back room with Gwen when she heard a customer come in. She went out to the counter, wiping her hands on her apron.

"*Bonjour, Monsieur,*" she said. The customer was a smartly dressed man in his forties. Pippa couldn't place him, but knew she'd seen him before.

He ordered a baguette, "*plutôt cuite*" and a slice of apple tart. She called out to Gwen who had just taken a fresh batch of loaves out of the oven, and brought one out. He took the hot bread appreciatively, then inserted some coins into the automated till. It switched from blue to green when he'd finished.

"Jackpot," he said. They smiled.

"Haven't we met?" Pippa asked. "Did I see you at Craig Barton's funeral perhaps?"

"I'm Jean-Michel," he replied. "I'm on the council, one of Mathieu's deputies. We are still waiting to find out who killed Craig. He was a good man."

"You mean for trying to stop the wind turbine project?"

"He was not alone, of course. You knew Didier? He tried to stop them too before he was killed. The turbines are the size of tower blocks looming over our little houses. Who will want to live here once the streets have been dug up for their cables? Not all you English who like it so much here."

"I wouldn't like one next to my house, that's for sure," Pippa said.

"You know what I think?" said Jean-Michel. "The police don't want to find who killed them."

Pippa remembered her promise to Yann but her natural curiosity pressed her on. "Why?"

"Because it could be embarrassing for the powers that be," he said, darkly. "Craig and Didier were both involved in getting up a petition to stop the wind farm. Now they are both dead. Do you think that's a coincidence? The council voted against them but the prefect allowed the project to continue through. There's democracy for you!"

"And you voted against Mathieu?" Pippa asked.

"Yes I did. So I'm in a difficult position now in the elections. How can I run on Mathieu's list when we have such a fundamental difference of opinion?"

"I imagine you're not the only one in this predicament, from what I've heard," said Pippa. "Craig's wife Meredith is planning to run. Might you consider switching sides?"

She could see she'd caught his interest.

"Is she?" he said. "It depends if she's going to campaign on the wind farm issue. Mathieu doesn't even mention onshore wind in his programme. *Putain!*"

Jean-Michel was about to say more when another customer came in. He picked up the bread and pastry and murmured "*Bon après-midi*" before turning to leave.

* * *

Pippa was still thinking about their conversation when she returned home that evening. After a light supper, consisting of smoked salmon salad followed by Camembert with a slice of crusty baguette, she took out her laptop.

She researched the arguments laid down in the protesters' petition. They were opposed to the project on the grounds of health, noise, environmental damage and danger to wildlife, as well as the devaluation of land and property. Pippa resolved to put Meredith in touch with Jean-Michel about the campaign.

Feeling tired, she went upstairs to set the alarm for 4 a.m. If she was in bed before 9.30 p.m. she felt fresh enough to cope with the day. She'd got used to watching the sun rise over the hills from behind her bakery and seeing the moment when the red lights on top of the wind farm turbines went out.

As she brushed her hair while sitting on the bed, there was still one question on her mind: how exactly could the deaths of both Craig and Didier be linked to the wind farm? She wondered whether to mention her chat with Jean-Michel to Yann but thought better of it.

Their relationship had quickly become intimate after their first proper kiss at the end of their *moules marinières* evening more than a month ago. But they only rarely spent the night together because of her crazy hours.

At least they'd been able to take advantage of the little spare time that their jobs allowed them. Yann had driven her to the seaside, only an hour away, and to visit local places of interest, all bereft of tourists at this time of year.

When Jennifer had suggested taking him round to dinner, she'd accepted on Yann's behalf. She'd only needed to reassure him that both Jennifer and Jonathan spoke French for him to agree. They'd set the dinner date for the following weekend.

They were bound to like him, she thought. She snuggled down under the duvet and pulled it up to her chin before switching off the bedside light and falling into a deep sleep.

CHAPTER 38: LUKE

"You look nice," said Jonathan.

Jennifer acknowledged the compliment. She'd finally gone to the hairdresser in Carhaix who had given her a "freshen up" that afternoon.

They were both standing at the sink preparing dinner for Pippa and Yann. It was just like the old days, when each of them had a purpose without having discussed it. He was peeling and scraping vegetables while she got to work on the chopping board.

"What time are they coming?" he asked.

"Not till just after eight. Pippa has to close up the bakery at half past seven. But we'll have to feed the kids first."

"I'm on it," he said. "I'll do them spaghetti in five minutes when I've finished this. What about nibbles?"

"I prepared something earlier while you were working," she said. "It's that puff pastry thing, *soleil* they call it because the tendrils of pastry intertwined with pesto look like a sun."

"I love that," he said.

"Yeah and it's so easy. It's warming in the oven."

* * *

The children finished their dinner in record time and went upstairs. While Jonathan was clearing up and setting the table in the living room, Jennifer went up to shower and get changed. Humming to herself, she put on some fake pearl earrings and her smartest trousers with a blouse. She also swapped her slippers for a pair of shoes. She hadn't met Pippa's gendarme friend before and didn't want him to think they were country bumpkins. On her way downstairs, she peered into Luke's bedroom. He seemed out of sorts and was sitting on the bed, fidgeting and staring into space. It was not like him.

She went in and sat next to him.

"What's up, little man?"

He grabbed her and buried his head in her chest.

"I know a secret," he whispered. "It was Mariam who let out the chickens."

He looked up at her, uncertain how she was going to react.

"And how do you know that?" She spoke as calmly as possible, trying not to show her alarm.

"She told me. But she said not to tell anybody."

Jennifer struggled to stop herself marching out of the room to confront her daughter.

"Just a second, this happened on Christmas Day, remember? Why are we only finding out now, two months later?"

"Because she only just told me!" he protested.

She took a deep breath and gave Luke a long hug. "You did the right thing to tell me. Did she say why she did it?"

"Because she saw Daddy with Romy's mummy in Carhaix on Christmas Eve. Mummy — are you getting a divorce?"

Could this be true? Jennifer felt as though her heart would burst from Jonathan's betrayal. Had he ever ended his relationship with Emma? She twisted Luke on the bed so that they could look into each other's eyes. His were damp with tears.

"Nobody's leaving, Luke. Don't you worry about it. I'll make sure that Mariam knows that too. We love you." She hoped her trembling voice didn't betray her emotion. She would have continued but heard the doorbell ring downstairs. Jonathan called up, "They're here!"

She gave Luke a final hug, blew him a kiss from the doorway and went downstairs, where Jonathan was hanging up the coats in the hall.

CHAPTER 39: THE DINNER PARTY

Pippa came in first, in a loose-fitting dress. Yann stood behind her wearing a navy-blue Breton sweater over a pair of pressed jeans.

Pippa seemed nervous as she said, "This is Yann. Jennifer, Jonathan," She gestured to the two others who shook Yann by the hand.

"*Entrez, entrez,*" said Jonathan. He ushered them into the living room where the fire crackled.

Yann sat down on the sofa and said straight away in English, "My English is very poor, I am sorry."

"You'll have to put up with our French, then," said Jennifer, using the *vous* form.

"*On peut se tutoyer,*" he replied, inviting them to call him by the more familiar term. But instead of relaxing her, the invitation had the opposite effect. She wished they would go home and leave her alone.

"Well, now, what would everyone like to drink?" she asked.

"I'm driving so I'll stick to water," said Yann.

"Oh yes, you wouldn't want to be stopped for drink driving, on the way home," said Jonathan. Jennifer didn't know whether to laugh, as they weren't used to socialising with a policeman.

She went into the kitchen in search of the drinks which she put on a tray. She was so angry after what she'd just heard that she felt like smashing the glasses against the kitchen wall. But she re-emerged with a forced smile on her face, before going back to collect the puff pastry *soleil* which attracted "oohs" from Pippa.

The evening passed awkwardly. The English felt strange speaking in French to each other, and occasionally lapsed into English, forgetting Yann's presence, before apologising to him.

The main course was duck breast which Jennifer realised was probably too well done for Yann's taste, despite his compliments.

The conversation kept coming back to a comparison of things British and French in which Yann insisted in all seriousness that the French were superior, in everything from cuisine to the punctuality of trains.

"But what about tea?" Pippa chipped in. "Why, oh why do the French serve tea with hot milk?"

Yann looked flummoxed. *Didn't everyone?* he seemed to be thinking.

"Yes, and what about kettles? Why don't the French use them?" Jennifer added.

Yann grinned. "But we make better coffee," he countered.

"Touché," said Jennifer. "But this isn't a competition, we're just teasing you." She didn't want him to feel they were ganging up on him on their first meeting. Yann turned to Jonathan to rekindle the conversation.

"I hear you work in finance," he said.

"I do when I can get the internet to work here," Jonathan replied.

"And in what sector exactly?"

"I do a bit of everything now that I work for myself. I do market analysis and I also advise my clients on investments, managing their portfolio, that sort of thing. When I worked in London, I was a financial adviser with a big City firm."

"And is that easy, watching the markets from the middle of Brittany?" Yann seemed genuinely puzzled.

"It's fine. I'm an hour ahead of London, which is OK for the Asian markets, and six hours ahead of New York. The only trouble is that it means a very long day for me, which is not ideal, because we have to get up early to feed the animals."

Jennifer wasn't even listening. He might have been reciting the weather forecast for all she knew. She was staring at Jonathan thinking, *How could you do this to me, you lying bastard?*

She realised that everyone's eyes were on her and that she was expected to reply to something that the Lying Bastard had said.

"Oh, can you excuse me a moment?" she said, putting down her knife and fork. "I just need to check something."

She disappeared into the kitchen where she sobbed silently at the kitchen sink until she could bring herself under control. She'd been combing through her memory, thinking back to Christmas Eve. She'd dropped Mariam off in Carhaix where everything was open for last-minute shopping, and she was supposed to meet up with Pervenche. Jonathan had gone into town in the afternoon, saying he needed to find something for the children's Christmas stockings, so he was the one who brought Mariam home. How had Mariam seemed? Sullen, yes, but no more than usual. Mariam had obviously not challenged Jonathan on the spot but had waited until she was left alone in the house the next day to exact her revenge.

Jennifer shook her head and dabbed her eyes with a tea towel. Then she took her apple crumble from the oven and left it on the counter before returning to the fray. She noticed the Lying Bastard glancing at her to check that she was OK. She glowered at him. She hoped he would realise that she was not OK. Not at all.

"I was just telling them about how we lost a young sheep and a lamb, and that was tough, wasn't it?" He reached over and tried to take her hand, which she withdrew to his obvious surprise. "But since then, our other ewe gave birth to two lambs. So it's nature's way of making us realise that in the midst of disaster there's hope. I mean there's a constant renewal . . . does that make any sense?"

Yann stopped chewing his last bite of duck breast. "I think you've put that very well," he said. "Do you keep ducks?"

"Oh no, these are bought ones, I'm afraid," Jennifer said. "But the potatoes and beans are ours. Next time I'll roast one of our chickens for you." By the time they'd finished pudding, the exchanges had become more strained. The prolonged conversation in French, which ventured into areas where their vocabulary was shaky, began to feel like an exam.

Yann asked the Lying Bastard what he thought about bitcoin.

"Crypto? Too risky for me," he replied. He turned to Jennifer. "How do you say I wouldn't touch them with a bargepole, in French?"

She shrugged. She no longer had any interest in this conversation and poured herself some more wine, without offering any to the others. Pippa began doing elaborate gestures involving an imaginary pole, making Yann even more confused.

"Oh never mind," the Lying Bastard said in the end. "Do you invest, then?" he asked Yann.

"No," came the reply.

They moved back to the sofa after dinner, while Jonathan went into the kitchen to make coffee.

"How's the bakery going?" Jennifer asked Pippa, knowing the answer perfectly well but trying to keep the conversation going. By now Yann had lapsed into silence, a glazed look in his eyes.

"Oh, I forgot to tell you," Pippa said. "I've got an Instagram account now. It's called @breadinBritanny."

"Oh, let's see," said Jennifer. Pippa pulled out her phone and scrolled through the pictures.

"These *Tropéziennes* cakes do really well. I guess because they're a bit different from the local fare, and they're a bit special," she said.

"That's a nice one of you," said Jennifer, pointing to a photo of Pippa behind the counter, her hair tied back with a ribbon.

"I've got more than nine hundred followers already," said Pippa. "Including my bakery tutor!"

The Lying Bastard attempted to draw out Yann by broaching the investigations into the Louennec murders. He replied politely enough but clearly didn't want to talk about it.

"Peeper thinks I have more influence in the *gendarmerie* than in reality," he smiled.

"But do you know what leads are being followed up about Craig Barton?"

Yann paused for thought for a moment before replying. "Was he killed because of his role on the council? Or because of his role in his association opposing the turbines? Or because he was an Englishman? This is what the magistrate is trying to establish," he said. He seemed to think he had already said too much because he changed the subject.

"Have you been to the Vallée des Saints?" he asked. "Peeper and I went there recently."

"I want to go back with my easel. If you don't know it, there's a great view over the Monts d'Arée," said Pippa. Jennifer looked at her watch as discreetly as possible. Pippa continued, "You must go. It's like a kind of Breton Easter Island, they've sculpted loads of granite statues, representing Breton saints, on a hill."

Finally, Yann placed a hand on Pippa's arm. "Shall we leave? It's getting late and I know you like to get to bed early."

She smiled and got up immediately. "Yes, I'm sorry, but you know how it is with my new job . . . this is a late night for me already."

"Of course. We have to get up early too." Jennifer jumped up and went to look for Pippa's coat. "Well, see you soon," she said. "I miss you on the market, you know."

"Me too. Let's get a coffee in the next couple of days." Pippa kissed her and Jonathan on the cheeks. "Three times in Brittany, apparently," she said in English with a glance at Yann. "Thanks so much for a lovely evening."

"Thank you," said Yann, also in English, before holding out his hand stiffly. "Nice to meet you."

Jennifer double locked the door behind them and turned to face the Lying Bastard. They went back into the living room where he grabbed a half empty bottle of Crozes-Hermitage and set it down on the coffee table with two glasses.

"I'm sorry you found the evening with your friend so difficult," he said. He sat on the sofa and patted a place next to him, but she ignored his invitation. She sat in an armchair to keep her distance. "What on earth was eating you tonight?"

"What's eating me? It's you, you rat! Do you realise that you are destroying our family!" She poured herself a glass of the wine and took a long swig.

"What!" Jonathan looked stunned. "What is all this about?"

"I don't suppose you're aware that it was Mariam who opened the chicken run on Christmas Day?"

"Mariam? What the . . . ? Why would she want to hurt us by doing a thing like that?"

He went to get up. "Sit down!" she ordered loudly. "It's late. Don't you dare go up there. We'll talk to her in the morning, together. And by the way, it's not her that wants to hurt us. It's obviously a cry for help. *You're* the one that's hurting her, you liar."

He caught hold of her arm and gripped her wrist.

"You're drunk," he said. "Stop making things up."

She shook herself free.

"Can't you see? She was already abandoned once in that refugee camp. So imagine how she must feel being rejected again by you! And Luke feels the same way too, by the way."

Jonathan shrank into the sofa, his eyes fixed on her like a trapped animal, but said nothing.

"You told me it was over with Emma! But Mariam saw you in Carhaix together on Christmas Eve and must have seen enough to make her realise that our marriage is collapsing.

Luke asked me tonight whether we're going to divorce." She burst into angry tears. "And you said you were going shopping for Christmas presents. Ha!

"So I'm going to give you one more chance, although God knows you don't deserve it. Do you choose her or your family? Your children are paying a price with their mental health because of your shenanigans. And frankly I don't know whether I'll ever trust you again, you lying bastard!"

He maintained his stunned silence. Jennifer got up and walked towards the stairs, saying over her shoulder, "Right, well, all I can say is that you're back on the sofa from now on. Maybe that will help you come to your senses."

He got up to follow her, but she turned on him.

"And don't you follow me!" she snarled. "Good night."

CHAPTER 40: AN UNRAVELLING

A sleepless night, clouded by alcohol, awaited Jennifer.

She was tormented by Jonathan's deception and the effect on Mariam. She also felt embarrassed by her own behaviour at dinner. How could she have been so unwelcoming and rude to their guests? What would Yann have thought of her? But worse, she was increasingly losing sight of how they could glue their family back together again.

It was still dark when she awoke at 7.30 a.m. and couldn't remember whether it was her turn to feed the animals. Unconsciously she reached across the bed for comfort then remembered that she'd banished Jonathan to the sofa again. She sighed, stretching out under the duvet. The house was silent. She wondered who to approach first, dreading the conversations that needed to be had.

She picked up her dressing gown and put on her slippers before crossing the hall to Mariam's room. She opened the door without knocking. Mariam was asleep, curled up in the bed. She closed the door again without a sound and crept downstairs, feeling like a stranger in her own house.

Byron wagged his tail lethargically when he saw her. She didn't even look in Jonathan's direction when she switched on the downstairs light and went straight into the kitchen to feed the dog and make herself a nice strong coffee.

She'd given Byron his arthritis pills and was staring out of the window into the darkness when she heard Jonathan clearing his throat behind her.

"Are you making coffee?" *Was it not obvious?*

She took out two mugs from the cupboard and set them on the table where she poured out the coffee. He helped himself to milk from the fridge and they sat down together.

"What do you want to do?" he asked in a quiet and solemn voice.

"Me? What do I want to do?" she said. "I think we've gone beyond that, haven't we? I mean this is now an existential question about whether our marriage is already dead and our family beyond help."

"Don't exaggerate," he said. "You pushed me away."

Jennifer hadn't heard this angle before. "Did I?"

"Yes. For months. How am I supposed to react when I'm forced to sleep on the sofa after a minor infidelity that I had ended myself, precisely in order to keep our family together."

The words *minor infidelity* penetrated her brain like a surgeon's knife.

"OK, so then the question is, what do *you* want?" She couldn't bring herself to call him by his name and was afraid she would blurt out "lying bastard" again.

"Honestly?" he said. "I'm prepared to give it another go, for the sake of the children."

"Well, thank you for recognising the damage you've done to our particularly vulnerable child, who was so upset that she let our chickens out!"

"Yes. I understand. I'm sorry I reacted like I did last night." His voice sounded genuinely apologetic.

"Toast?"

He didn't seem to understand what she meant. After a moment he nodded and got up. "I'll make some."

They busied themselves, setting the table.

"So to ask my question again," said Jonathan, sitting down. "What do you want to do?"

She buttered herself a slice of toasted baguette and spread marmalade on top. With a sip of hot coffee it was so comforting.

"Of course I want to keep our family together. But you'll really have to stop seeing your lover, assuming that you still are."

He said nothing. His crestfallen look was impossible to read.

"I mean it," Jennifer went on. "And I want you to go up right now to Mariam and apologise. You must give her a hug and tell her and Luke that we love them and we're not going to abandon them."

She watched him, still in bare feet and wearing his T-shirt and shorts, climb the stairs to make peace with their children.

CHAPTER 41: A "DARK SECRET"

"Is everything OK?" Pippa asked Jennifer.

Pippa had suggested meeting at the Central Café on her day off, no doubt sensing that something was wrong.

"I'm so sorry, I wanted to apologise for my rude behaviour on Saturday. I'm so embarrassed," said Jennifer. "It's not an excuse but just before you arrived I discovered that it was Mariam who opened the gate to the chicken run on Christmas Day."

"Oh no! Why? Was it a cry for help?" Pippa reached out to stroke Jennifer's arm. "And why did you only find out now?"

Jennifer sighed. "She saw Emma and Jonathan together on Christmas Eve and so I suppose she wanted to punish us, or him at least. And the lying bastard, or LB as I shall now call him, had told me their affair was over!"

Pippa's sympathy only served to make Jennifer more upset. "The worst thing is, though, that she confided in Luke, and he was the one who told me. Mariam said yesterday that she waited until she couldn't keep it secret any longer. What gets me is that she must have been observing us, worried about us breaking up, for a whole two months!"

"Oh God." Pippa blew a little hole into the froth on top of her coffee and took a sip.

"Yes. And what I don't know is whether it's something deeper than just worrying that we're going to split up. Luke is very upset. It's the rejection, of course. They feel they're to blame."

"And Mariam's so vulnerable," said Pippa.

"Exactly." Jennifer finished her espresso in one gulp and pushed it away.

"And what did you tell them?"

"We wanted to reassure them, obviously. But Mariam's smart, she must have noticed the tension between us. And no doubt Jonathan's disappearances at odd times. Anyway, we've both told them, separately, that they're our priority and that we're staying together. What else could we say?"

She looked over at Pippa. "The thing is though, that he's betrayed my trust. Not once, but twice! Mariam was walking along to the supermarket where he was supposed to pick her up, and passed this café where she saw them sitting holding hands. Actually it feels weird to be here now."

She gave a bitter laugh. Pippa got up from her plastic chair and moved onto the bench to sit next to Jennifer.

"I'm so sorry," she said. "But of course you're right to want to keep the family together. I'm sure that Mariam really needs her father at the moment."

Jennifer nodded. "You're dead right about that. As for that home-wrecking divorcee, if ever I see her again, there's going to be another murder in this village."

She leaned back. "Anyway. I liked Yann. Although if we were to do it again, I think I'd invite Derek and Solenn, so he'd have a bit of company. It was unfair of us to invite him as the only French guest."

Pippa smiled. "Next time," she said. "Or maybe I'll have them over with you for a return match. They're a nice couple. It's just a shame about the timing, I guess."

"Yann didn't give away much about the investigation, did he?" Jennifer commented.

"I don't really think he wants to talk about it with us. I thought it was interesting though when he mentioned the theories."

"Yes, but I'd have thought they'd have been working on that basis from the very start!"

Pippa rested her hands on her chin and stared at Jennifer.

"Do you know, I'm starting to believe that Didier and Craig were killed because of their anti-wind turbine campaign."

"Really?" said Jennifer. "You've got evidence?"

"Not directly. That's the problem." She mentioned her conversations with Didier's widow and the deputy mayor at the bakery.

"Anyway, I told Yann about what I heard from Nathalie, and I'm pretty confident that he's going to follow up. Fingers crossed, anyway."

Jennifer smiled. "That's good. That poor old lady, being subjected to that sort of abuse."

"Yes. Not only that, but Jean-Michel from the council sounded open to switching to Meredith's electoral list over the wind farm project. I spoke to her about going big on that in her platform, which might swing votes her way."

"Great," said Jennifer. She found the distraction was helping her to feel more like herself again than playing the role of the wronged wife.

"OK, so in the absence of any progress in the police investigation — as far as we're aware — what do we know so far?" Pippa began. "Number one, Adam drowns after being blackmailed by a client over a house he sold him. Let's call it a separate incident because I can't see any connection to the others, apart from maybe anti-Brit sentiment."

Jennifer nodded. "Let's not lose sight of that aspect," she said.

"Next, Didier is pushed into the slurry tank — possibly by those two guys with some connection to the developers. Then — Craig is killed — presumably by someone he knows. So, the question is — is there a connection between Didier's death and Craig's murder?"

"Who knows?" said Jennifer. "But if we take account of what your customer mentioned, it could be that Craig was killed because he'd found out a dark secret."

"I'm with you," Pippa replied. "But wait a sec. What about Mathieu's effigy? Who hoisted the sex doll onto the turbine?"

Jennifer smiled. "As Craig would say, *Cui bono*? It must have been one of the protesters. But we're talking about murder."

"OK, so what do we do now?"

"The first thing is to keep in touch with that deputy mayor, in case he finds out anything more. So, you'd better make sure you keep on baking those baguettes the way he likes them!"

"He also had an apple tart. Anyway, the bakery is only across the street from the *mairie*."

"You see . . ."

"Don't remind me . . . I've got to go in later to prep for tomorrow, even on a Monday." Pippa groaned and reached for her handbag to pay the bill.

Jennifer looked at her phone. "I've got to go too. But let's keep in touch on this. And make sure that Yann keeps an ear to the ground!"

CHAPTER 42: THE CAMPAIGN

Meredith was waiting by her front door when Jennifer drove up to the house.

Captain raced out of his kennel and began circling her. She stopped dead while Meredith pointed to the kennel until the dog slunk out of the way.

They went into the dining room where Emma was sitting at the table draining a mug of tea. She got up, quickly. Jennifer couldn't bring herself to say hello.

"Oh hi, Jennifer," said Emma. "I hear you've come to help Mum with her campaign."

"Yes."

Emma looked as young and nubile as ever. Had Jonathan already told her their relationship was really over? Jennifer wondered.

Emma picked up her keys from the table. "I'm just leaving actually," she said. "I've got to pick up Romy."

Jennifer waited while Meredith accompanied her daughter to the door. She noticed photos of Craig and his family on top of an old-fashioned sideboard. She heard Meredith say, "Drive carefully," and realised that Emma must have parked her car round the corner outside the garage. Had she known she risked bumping into her, she'd have stayed at home.

"Well," said Meredith, returning to the room. "There's still some tea left, if you'd like some?"

Jennifer took Emma's place beside a pile of papers at one end of the dining table. Meredith poured them both a cup of tea from the tea pot and fetched some *galettes bretonnes* from a packet.

So is Emma helping with the campaign as well? Jennifer wondered. She was starting to plot her escape from this chore.

"Oh no. Actually, she thinks that I should stay out of politics, after what happened to Craig. I asked you because you've got a professional background, you know what's needed."

She chewed on a biscuit and pointed at the documents. "These are some of Craig's papers that I dug out while I was doing my research," she said. "I've not had time to go through everything yet, but this will do. These are some from the anti-wind farm association."

"Ah, that's interesting," said Jennifer. "So you're going to put the turbines in your campaign?"

"Yes. I've already spoken to one of the deputy mayors about it. Pippa called me about him. It's what Craig would have wanted," she said. Her voice began to tremble. Jennifer patted her hand and gave her a moment before continuing.

"We'll need a profile pic of you. And what's your slogan?" Jennifer asked. "How about 'wind of change'?"

"That's good, but maybe too good," said Meredith. "I wouldn't want to put the wind up them." Jennifer smiled. "I mean, in a rural area like this, that could be seen as a bit aggressive. Too pushy."

"Too pushy?"

"You know what they're like here," she said. "Even though I'm French and I've lived here for ages, they still see me as a foreigner. It's complicated."

"So, what are you thinking?"

"I thought something like, *Avec Vous*. It's unifying, do you see what I mean? Working together. Macron's alliance used '*Ensemble*' in the elections, it's the same sort of thing."

"OK, that works for me," said Jennifer. "Have you done the rest of the text for the flyers?"

"One sec." Meredith opened her laptop and called up a file. "See here," she said. "I was thinking on the front there'd be a picture of me — maybe in front of the church? — saying '*Meredith Barton, Avec Vous*'. And then put a short bio about me with the bullet points of my programme. More transparency, stop the wind turbines, stimulating *la vie associative*, that sort of thing. Oh, and I think I should mention Craig, don't you? Because I'm doing this in his name, really."

"I like it," said Jennifer. "Do you get any allowance for your campaign literature?"

"I'm afraid not. I have to pay for everything myself. I'll be pushing these through people's letterboxes. The *commune* is too small to get any financial contribution."

"Don't worry, we can help you out with the distribution," said Jennifer. "I can hand out some at the market too."

"Thank you."

"Cool," said Jennifer, getting up. "Tell me, when do you need this by?"

"In the next week or so if possible. Is that OK?"

"It'll be tight but I'm sure we can manage. Email me your text as soon as it's ready. I'll see if my printer guy in town will give you a deal."

CHAPTER 43: FLYERS

The days were getting longer at last. March was planting season in the smallholding and it was back-breaking.

Jennifer stood up from her crouched position where she and Jonathan, aka LB, were planting onion sets after the children got bored and returned to the house. She stretched her back, putting her hands on her hips. A black shape swooped low in the direction of the barn before disappearing out of sight.

"Oh look! Do you think that's a swallow?" she called out. A couple of them had nested in a mud-encased nest under the eaves the previous spring.

"Not necessarily," said Jonathan. "There are fewer of them every year, so I hear. Drought in Africa, pesticides here, you name it. How are you doing?"

"Not so bad. I've almost finished these but it's too late to start on sowing the carrots tonight, don't you think?"

By now, they'd been in Louennec long enough to know what worked in their soil and what didn't. Asparagus, for example, needed a sandy soil and would not flourish. But their artichoke plants in contrast produced up to ten artichokes each.

"What do you think about going home at Easter to see my mum?" he asked, knocking the soil from his trowel.

She'd wondered when he was going to mention this with the approach of the school holidays. But a family holiday with mother-in-law was the last thing she wanted.

"We could try. But it's a busy time here, and we'd need to get someone to look after the animals, water the plants and so on, wouldn't we? Not to mention Byron." She added, "Maybe you should go. I can manage here."

He didn't respond immediately. Then he said, "That might make sense. But what about the kids?"

"Mariam's already asked me about going away with Pervenche and her parents. I don't have a problem with that, do you?"

"I suppose you would have mentioned it to me eventually, wouldn't you?" She sensed the irritation in his voice. This was how they communicated these days. She realised she had to take her share of blame, but *he* was the lying bastard, wasn't he?

"That leaves Luke," she said, ignoring his tone. "So you could either take him with you, or he could stay here with me. I'm sure he's got plenty projects in the garden he could get on with."

"OK. Leave it for now," he said. "Maybe we'll go and visit Mum in the summer, we can plan ahead. She's always travelling anyway."

They put the tools away in the barn and were about to return to the house when Jennifer's phone rang.

"Oh great," she said. "That was the printer. I've time to pick up the flyers from Carhaix now, haven't I?"

"Sure," he said. "I'll get Mariam to help in the kitchen. She'll enjoy that," he added, sarcastically.

* * *

"Shall we have a look?" Jonathan asked. He gestured towards the cardboard box containing Meredith's flyers.

"What is it?" Luke asked.

"Finish your ice cream," Mariam said. "It's Romy's granny who's running for mayor."

"So will she be famous?" he asked.

"She won't be on TikTok if that's what you mean," said Jennifer. "It's a local election, in the *commune*. She wants to replace Craig who died." She remembered her conversation about death with Luke on the day of the funeral, but he didn't react. "With a bit of luck she'll get in."

Luke ate the remaining two spoonfuls of his vanilla ice cream, then said, "Please may I leave the table?" They all laughed at his politeness. He pushed his chair away from the table and went upstairs.

"Me too," said Mariam and headed up to her room.

"Thanks for setting the table," Jonathan called after her.

"You're welcome."

Jennifer stood up and went to pick up a knife to open the box. She took out a couple of the flyers and handed one to Jonathan.

"Nice picture," he said. Jennifer had taken Meredith standing in front of the church bell tower. The entrance to the village hall could be seen nearby. She was looking straight into the camera with a firm gaze to show that she meant business. The headline said: "*Votez Meredith Barton. Avec vous à Louennec*".

He turned over the brochure and ran through her profile, in which she said that her career as a teacher had made her want to give something back to people in need. She went on to explain that she wanted to continue Craig's legacy after making Louennec their family home.

"That's nice," he commented.

Then he read the main points of her programme, and frowned.

"Did you read this?" he said.

"Er, yes. Why?" The implicit criticism made her feel insecure.

"Did she tell you that she's top of a list of candidates? I thought she's running as an independent."

"She is, but she's hooked up with a couple of ecologists and other independents who were already on the council under the slogan *Avec Vous*. In fact she's stolen some of the councillors on his list, including a deputy mayor. What's wrong with that?"

"Yes, but did she tell you she's top of her list? Isn't it obvious that she's setting up in opposition to Mathieu and co? He's got his own list because he wants to get re-elected."

"Yes, she did and so what? You know that he and Craig didn't get on," she said.

"Yes, but Craig is dead, isn't he?"

Jennifer said nothing, and looked down at the table. Maybe she could have edited Meredith's text, warned her, maybe, not waved it through in such a hurry. But the bottom line was that she agreed with what Meredith was saying. She didn't want their lovely village to be ruined by more wind turbines. One wind farm was quite enough.

"I just thought that she's lived here longer than us, she knows the locals . . ."

"I know. But look, when you read what she says about stopping the wind turbines, I mean it's a direct contradiction of what's been agreed on the council."

"But it isn't though. They took a vote and the mayor ignored the result! That's what Craig told Pippa!"

"And what about this bit?" He jabbed a finger at the pamphlet. "Talking about greater transparency? I know that's because of what happened to her neighbour and the orchard, but again it's like a direct attack on how Mathieu is running the place." He shook his head. "I just think that she could have put this in a less aggressive way."

"You may be right," said Jennifer. "But it is an election leaflet after all."

"Well, all I can say is that judging from my experience, they don't like foreigners coming along and telling them how to run things," said Jonathan. "Just ask Derek. He's married to a local and that's what he said to me the other day. On top of everything else, as you know, they blame us for the house prices going up."

He put down the flyer. "Look, I'm just saying that enough people in this village have already died. I don't want people to be at each other's throats, because things can get out of control."

"But everyone's already at each other's throats in this village, including us," she hit back. "We thought we were coming to an idyllic place in the middle of the French countryside, but look what happened? Killers are out there and they could strike again!"

CHAPTER 44: RUMOURS

"How's it going, Meredith?"

Meredith loomed into view, clad in her voluminous cape, as Jennifer was packing up her market stall. She'd sold all her eggs, lettuces and potatoes, and every broiler except one which she needed to deliver to a private customer.

Meredith waved a handful of pamphlets and came over. She was still limping slightly and walked with a cane.

"Not so bad. I've been meeting a lot of people, they seem really open to voting for me. A lot knew Craig because of his work on the council, so that's good. And thanks for helping out."

Jennifer had taken Mariam with her after school a few days earlier to deliver the pamphlets to outlying houses where she'd jumped out of the car and pushed them through the letterbox. Jennifer had listened in silence to her running commentary about how pesticides were killing the bees as they drove past fields of rapeseed.

"You're very welcome," Jennifer replied to Meredith. "Do you remember saying you didn't want to be too pushy? I'm wondering about the wisdom of you running as head of your list."

"Well, put it this way, I was persuaded to by the councillors who came over to my side from Mathieu's list. I was flattered, I suppose."

Jennifer wrinkled her nose. "I hope it doesn't cause problems for the rest of us, that's all. Jonathan was saying the locals don't like Brits trying to run things."

Meredith raised herself to her full height, leaning on her cane. "Look, Jennifer, I can tell you that I've just as much right to run for mayor as the next person here. Don't forget that I'm French, thanks to having dual nationality, even though I'll always be a Brit as far as the villagers are concerned. Of course, when the UK was still in the EU, I could have stood in the local election anyway, but Brexit changed all that."

She sighed, before continuing, "Let's face it, if our little expat community wasn't here, Louennec wouldn't be the thriving little village that it is now. It would have been completely abandoned! Look at Pippa, reviving the bakery. That's made a huge difference. Before that it was going to rack and ruin."

"You're right, I'm sorry. I just wanted to double-check that you're going into this with your eyes open. What about the flyers?" said Jennifer. "I managed to hand out this morning the rest of the last batch you gave me. I'll take some more if you like."

Meredith dug into a tote bag and gave her about twenty pamphlets. "Will this do? I've almost run out!

"By the way," she added. "You know the woman in the village who lives with her stepsons?"

"The one on the corner of the main street?"

"That's the one, yes. I knocked on her door when I was out canvassing, and when she eventually opened the door she was acting strangely."

"Strangely? How?" Jennifer asked.

"Well, nervous really. She kept looking behind her as though she was frightened. You know her stepsons are staying there, don't you? I thought maybe one of them was there, so I asked if she was OK and she said yes. But I'm sure she's not. Anyway, then I left, and I noticed there was a car in the drive, but I don't know if it's hers. Do you ever see her?"

"I can't say I do."

"I mean it's probably none of our business, but I just had this hunch that there's something nasty in the woodshed."

"Leave it with me. I think she's one of Pippa's customers," said Jennifer. She didn't mention what she'd already heard from Pippa and heaved the last of her boxes into her car boot. "You're getting feedback are you, about your candidacy?"

Meredith lowered her voice. "It's very interesting, actually. What I'm hearing is that Mathieu is really unpopular in the village. Craig had always complained about him, but now I know it's true!"

"Really? What are they saying?"

"I'm very glad I put the turbines at the top of my programme because the villagers I've spoken to are very worked up about it. They say that Mathieu is in the developers' pocket."

"Yes, but that could be just a rumour. I mean, can anyone prove it?" said Jennifer.

CHAPTER 45: A WARNING

About thirty people had filed into the *salle des fêtes* in Louennec to listen to the mayor.

There were just enough wooden chairs for them all to sit on. Mathieu stood at the front and surveyed his audience, with a nod of recognition here, mouthing *bonsoir* there, or a smile, like a rockstar. Pippa and Jennifer sat at the back to support Meredith who had taken out a notebook from her handbag.

Mathieu cleared his throat and began. "Thank you for coming, everyone. As you know I'm running for re-election with my team which has been working tirelessly for the residents of Louennec for the past six years. Let me tell you about our achievements, starting with the construction of this very hall under my administration, because we want to serve you for another term."

He went on to list how he had settled grievances which pitted farmers against residents living in the village centre, cleaned up the village pond "for the enjoyment of young and old", and ensured the reopening of a bakery.

Pippa wondered whether she'd heard correctly. She remembered how Mme Le Goff had tried to put her off taking the bakery lease, and now here they were claiming credit! She caught Jennifer's attention and rolled her eyes.

"What are you doing about our security, Mathieu?" somebody called out. A middle-aged man stood up near the back. "My grandchildren are terrified. I lost my farm hand and nobody's been arrested. One of your councillors was murdered before Christmas. An English estate agent was killed. And you don't even mention it!"

Pippa cast her eyes round the audience in case Yann was there, but she couldn't see him. Mathieu held up a hand to quieten things down. His moustache twitched slightly. He bore a striking resemblance to his effigy on the wind turbine.

"Armel, please, you know that we're not responsible for security in the village. I've already had a word with the *gendarmerie* about patrols and it's in hand. Is that what you're talking about?"

"I'm talking about finding the culprits and until that happens our families won't feel safe," the man grumbled, to applause from the gathering.

"Right, well, first of all, as you are aware, the estate agent's presumed killer is going to be put on trial very soon. Regarding your other allegations, my understanding is that the investigators are indeed making progress on one of the cases, but I can't go into details, obviously."

People in the audience began murmuring. Pippa dug Jennifer in the ribs. Then Mathieu returned to his prepared speech.

"In the last election, my list was unopposed," he said. "This time, however, we have competition from another list which is entirely focused on the future of wind farms around our *commune*. Our list is representative of the whole village, not a small bunch of activists." He raised his voice as he pronounced the last word with distaste.

"We have young and retired people, farmers, and white-collar workers who live in the village. I'm not ashamed to say that I was among those who voted in council in favour of the wind farm development."

"Yes, but you lost the vote, Mathieu." Everyone turned round to look at the speaker.

"I'm coming to that, Jean-Pierre," he replied. "I wanted to tell you that the reason I voted in favour is because we can't stick our heads in the sand. This debate is about our children's future. We need to move away from fossil fuels and this is the way forward. Anyway, I have no doubt that the project will eventually be approved."

"What about solar?" someone said.

"What about when there's no wind," said another voice.

He ignored them and pressed on.

"I maintain that our village can benefit from the small number of projects that have been proposed. We can reinvest in your future with the proceeds paid by the developers. As you know we are planning a new sports hall."

A young man with a pony tail was recognised. "What about offshore? I don't understand why we need wind farms here when they can be in the sea."

Mathieu nodded. "Thank you for asking this question," he said. "It's true that we need offshore wind to reach our climate targets. It is happening. But we still need to develop onshore."

Meredith put up her hand. "Yes, Marie," said Mathieu.

"Meredith," she corrected him. "Allow me to respond to you on a thing or two," she said, speaking very calmly in fluent but accented French. Referring to his "diverse" list of candidates, she said, "We are not a small bunch of activists. We have the benefit of experience thanks to the four councillors who have deserted you to run on our list, including one of your deputies!"

Mathieu's twisted face was a picture. Meredith went on: "But what I want to say is that I think there is some concern in this hall about our quality of life if these turbines are allowed to ruin our landscape. As you know there are complaints about the noise from residents who live close to turbines, their effect on the environment owing to their cement foundations and the danger to birds from their blades, not to mention the effects on livestock from their magnetic field."

A farmer jumped up before she could continue. "That's rubbish," he said. "There's no proof of anything that you're saying."

Jennifer noticed one villager could no longer contain himself. "Who benefits?" he shouted from his seat, waving an arm. "It's not us but the developers, and rich people like you!" He pointed at the previous speaker.

"And in any case it's all being decided from on high!" he went on before sitting down again. "We count for nothing!"

"Hold on, hold on," said Mathieu. He looked round the audience at the raised hands and nodded at a woman. "Yes, Madame."

"Monsieur Morel, you say the opposition list is totally focused on the turbines but they also say that they are campaigning for greater transparency at the *mairie*," she said. People began muttering again. "We didn't hear about the vote on the new local urban plan until it was too late to do anything about it!"

Jennifer wondered whether the woman was Meredith's neighbour who had lost the right to sell her orchard for housing development.

"Madame, all our meetings are open to the public. It's a matter of public record," said Mathieu. Some loud grumbling broke out in the hall.

Mathieu wound up the meeting shortly afterwards, and shook the hands of constituents who lined up to speak to him. Pippa and Jennifer waited outside for Meredith to emerge into the cold.

She was smiling.

"I'd say you did quite well out of that," said Jennifer.

"They seem to know who I am, don't they?"

"You're the official opposition!" said Pippa. "Well done!"

"Phew, yes, well, only a couple of weeks to go," said Meredith. "We'll see. Now I know why Craig got so excited about being elected. Mathieu is obviously a bit hot under the collar because of the councillors who defected from his list to join mine. And that's down to Craig."

* * *

The next evening, Jennifer's phone rang just as she was about to take a cauliflower cheese out of the oven.

"Can you get that?" she shouted to Jonathan, who picked up the phone in the living room. She heard him speaking to someone, listening in silence for a long while, then promising to go round after dinner.

"What's up?" she said, placing the hot dish on the kitchen table in front of the children who began helping themselves.

"That was Meredith. I'll tell you later." *This must be important*, she thought.

Once they'd finished eating and washed up, Jennifer went upstairs to let the children know that they'd be at Meredith's for a little while.

"I told you this would happen," Jonathan grumbled as they got into the car.

"Why, what's happened?"

"Meredith's campaigning has backfired," was all he would say. They pulled up by the dog kennel and rang the doorbell. She was waiting for them in her jacket and came outside.

"This way," she said. She led them along the drive flanked by molehills to her garage whose doors had been daubed with red paint. The letters said: "*Rosbifs* Go Home".

CHAPTER 46: GOING VIRAL

They stared at the message in silence until Meredith said, "Who would do this?"

"Should I contact the police?" she asked. "I mean this is so shocking."

Jennifer looked at Jonathan, who replied, "You could, I suppose. But I don't think you'd get very far."

"Yes, but that's not the point, is it?" Jennifer protested. "Wait, though, I think you could take advantage of this in your campaign. We can get ahead of it. I mean, it doesn't have to be negative, you can hit back."

Neither of them could see what she meant. Meredith offered them a cup of tea but Jonathan said they had to get back.

"Lock all your doors, Meredith," said Jonathan in a stern voice. "We don't know whether this could escalate into more extremist violence before the election."

Jennifer shot him a fierce look. Why did Meredith need to be more scared than she was already?

"Let me come back with my camera tomorrow, OK, Meredith? I think *Le Télégramme* might be interested in covering this as a campaign story," she said.

Meredith still looked puzzled. "You mean this could be some free publicity?"

"That's exactly what I mean."

* * *

The next morning Jennifer returned and had Meredith pose in front of the damaged doors for a series of photos.

"This shows how vicious this campaign in our little village has got," said Meredith, who had put on a flowing dress for her close-up, and was wearing lipstick. "But it's not just French against English, it's also French against French, isn't it?"

"Well, yes. But this is definitely French against Brits. Can you point at the doors?" said Jennifer, crouching down. "And look angry. Thanks."

Jennifer finished taking the snaps within a few minutes, taking advantage of the natural light and Meredith's compliance. She stowed her camera in the car and prepared to leave. "I'm going to send this to the paper, and see if they want to assign a reporter. So we'll see!"

"Emma's furious by the way," said Meredith. "You remember she didn't want me to campaign in the first place? She says it sets neighbours against each other. But it's too late now."

It certainly is, Jennifer thought.

"Are you OK? I mean, are you worried about your personal safety after this?" she asked.

Meredith's hooded eyes flickered. "I'm nervous, yes, of course, because I'm living alone now. But also sad. I hadn't expected to be a hate crime target after living in Louennec for so many years."

The paper didn't waste any time in sending over a reporter to interview Meredith. When Jennifer checked the Louennec page of the paper online that evening she saw the headline: "The Englishwoman who wants to be mayor of Louennec". The article was a sympathetic profile of Meredith which mentioned her husband's murder, and in which she ruled out returning to England after seeing the xenophobic warning on her garage doors.

"I'm not going to fall into the trap that they set for me," she was quoted as saying. "The people of Louennec have made my family so welcome all the time we've lived here. It must be a tiny minority of villagers who can't see the contribution that we've made. And now I hope to take it a step further if a majority show their trust in me by electing my list."

The reporter asked whether she suspected this minority of being responsible for Craig's death. She cleverly avoided answering, saying that she didn't want to interfere with the investigation and was sure that his killer would soon be identified.

"Come and look at this," Jennifer called out to Jonathan. He came into the kitchen from the living room where he was watching Luke playing Clash Royale on his tablet. He always hoped for more than his strict half hour of video game time if his father joined in.

"Meredith's now a local celebrity and Mathieu's going to be furious!" she said.

He read it over her shoulder. "This is good," he commented. "I think she's going to get elected. But she missed an opportunity to complain about the police."

"Just a sec though," said Jennifer, pointing to a paragraph in the article. "The reporter's done his homework." The article explained that Craig had been shot during the dress rehearsal of an "English farce" by someone "from outside the hall".

"That's more than we knew, isn't it? They must have examined the video that Meredith shot. At least they're making progress. That's what the mayor said."

The next morning Meredith called to say the Paris correspondent of the *Daily Telegraph* wanted to interview her.

"Give them hell," said Jennifer. "Let me know how it goes."

When Meredith called back, Jennifer was in her lab standing in chicken feathers.

"I felt that went really well," she said. "They were interested in the whole wind farm issue. I guess it resonates back home now, because of the Nimbyism about onshore wind farms. And they want to use your photo."

The published article had a headline that ran: "Englishwoman stands up to the French in municipal elections".

"Typical *Telegraph*," Jennifer grumbled, when she saw it.

CHAPTER 47: THE SCREAM

The sound of two foxes yelping in the garden woke Pippa in the middle of the night. She threw back the sheets and swore out loud when she saw the time: 2.15 a.m.

She went to the bathroom then returned to bed. But she tossed and turned, unable to get back to sleep, knowing that her alarm was going to ring in less than two hours.

She turned over in her mind her list of chores when she got to the bakery. These days, thanks to Gwen, it was running like a well-oiled machine. Her apprentice worked mainly in the back, mixing and shaping the dough which would be waiting for Pippa first thing in the morning in the fridge, ready for baking. Croissants could be kept in the proofing chamber. That ensured that the smell of freshly baked bread would greet their first customers at 8 a.m. Gwen had also suggested that they use a phone app to sell leftovers at a reduced price before closing in the evening. It was proving popular with young couples who worked in Carhaix and who picked up a bag of surprise goodies on their way home.

But the app had only increased their workload. Pippa had to recognise that the responsibility and stress was affecting her sleep. The more she tried to restore her energy, the worse it got. Her only day off was partly spent prepping for the next morning's bake. The enterprise could only be profitable if she kept a steady stream of batches in the oven. Here she was, a company boss and administrator rolled into one. She wished she could confide in someone, and bounce ideas off them. But who could she turn to? Not Yann, who'd never had a comparable job. Maybe someone like Mark, with his accounting experience? But she didn't know him well enough. Or Jonathan?

As she turned over in bed yet again to plump up the pillow, she heard loud shouting not far from the house. Pippa sat bolt upright and listened. That sound was definitely not sex-crazed foxes. She got up, opened the bedroom windows and pushed open the shutters. She could see a light on in Madame Briand's house.

While she was still wondering where the noise was coming from, she heard a man shouting followed by a high-pitched scream. It must be the old woman.

She looked for her phone. Yann needed to know about this. He answered after four rings.

"Oh thank goodness!" she said.

"What's the matter? Are you OK?" he asked.

"I just heard shouting and screaming coming from Madame Briand's house!" she cried. "I'm going straight round to see what's going on."

"Are you sure it's coming from their house?"

She hesitated. "Yes. No. I think so."

At that moment there was another scream, maybe a man's. "Did you hear that? I'm going round," she said.

"Peeper, listen to me. You are to stay here. This is my job and I'm the one who is going to the house. Do you understand?"

"OK," she said. She put on her dressing gown and went downstairs. A few minutes later, when she was peering through a crack in the blinds, she heard Yann's door slam and saw his silhouetted figure run past. She went back upstairs to see what she could discover from the window of her darkened bedroom. The lights in the house were still on. She waited, watching, her heart pumping. Nothing happened for about fifteen minutes.

Then she saw a flashing light outside the old woman's house. Yann must have alerted the *gendarmerie*. Unless it was an ambulance? The suspense was too much to bear.

She pulled on the first clothes that came to hand, slipped on her shoes, grabbed a jacket and ran down the street. An ambulance was parked outside the white fence. Just as she arrived at the corner of their street she saw two paramedics carrying a stretcher into the back.

A car marked *gendarmerie* was parked in front of the ambulance. Yann was talking to an officer. Another emerged from inside, gripping a middle-aged man. His face was illuminated by the light from inside the house. She held her breath as she recognised the person in a leather jacket who had given her a death stare when speeding away in his car.

She remembered Yann's instructions and retraced her steps home. It was now too late to even think about getting back to sleep. She went straight into the kitchen and made herself a bowl of strong coffee.

About half an hour later, when she was doodling on a sheet of paper, her front doorbell rang. It was Yann.

"I saw your light was on," he said. "You did the right thing to call me."

"What happened? Is the woman OK?"

"From what we could gather, one guy in the house took out a kitchen knife and stabbed the old lady, but another man, the other stepson it seems, also has stab wounds. They've both been taken to hospital. The medic said the guy with stab wounds has life-threatening injuries but Madame Briand will survive."

"And the attacker? He's been arrested?"

"Of course." Yann shook his head. "We questioned him about Didier only a few days ago, and he denied everything, of course. It looks like he might have taken it out on his stepmother."

Pippa gasped. "You mean because he thought she was the one who tipped off the *gendarmerie*?"

"I'm afraid so." He took a step towards her to comfort her, and gave her a kiss.

"Well, he's going to pay now, isn't he, the brute . . ." she said.

"Oh yes."

He turned to go and she opened the front door.

"It's late, you'd better get some sleep," she said.

"What about you?"

"There's no point in me going to bed now. My alarm is going to ring soon."

She closed the door behind him, and leaned on it heavily. She didn't want to accuse Yann, it wasn't his fault, but she felt responsible. They'd missed an opportunity to help this woman who hadn't wanted to be helped.

CHAPTER 48: POLLING DAY

Meredith had invited all the Louennec players to her house for an *apéro* on a fine spring evening which happened to be the first round of the municipal elections.

"This is absolutely my favourite time of year," said Jennifer. She turned round to admire Meredith's garden when she and Jonathan reached the door. Footpaths were bordered by daffodils and lilac blossom hung in the hedge.

Emma came out to greet them. She seemed nervous.

"Is anything wrong?" Jennifer asked. "Where's Meredith?"

"It's just that we'll know the result any minute," she said. "The polls closed at 6 p.m., and Mum is there, watching the count. She said it wouldn't take more than an hour, but I've not heard yet. Why don't you come in anyway?"

This is awkward. Jennifer glanced at Jonathan who showed no reaction. They stepped inside and hung up their jackets.

"But aren't there two rounds?" Jonathan asked.

"Yes, yes, of course. But often in small *communes* like ours it can be decided in the first round. I mean Mathieu swept the board with his list last time."

"Gosh," said Jennifer. "I wonder . . ."

Emma held up a hand. "Don't say anything, you'll jinx it!"

Derek was already seated on the sofa in the living room. Jennifer sat next to him, leaving Jonathan to find another chair while Emma disappeared into the kitchen.

"How's it going?" he said to Derek.

"Not so bad, and you?"

Jonathan nodded. *This is going to be a fun evening,* Jennifer thought. She hadn't expected to be spending so much time with Jonathan and his ex-mistress.

Emma returned with some glasses on a tray, and asked what they wanted to drink. "I don't think we'll have to wait more than a few minutes," she said. "Solenn is one of the *scrutateurs* doing the count."

"Is Romy here?" Jennifer asked her.

"No, the babysitter's at the house," she replied.

"Same with us," said Jennifer. "Who else is coming?"

"Mark's on the way. And Pippa. She's bringing sausage rolls."

The doorbell rang. "Maybe that's her," said Emma, going to the door.

She came back with Mark, who presented Emma with a bottle of gin.

"To drown your sorrows," he commented. Was that supposed to be funny? Jennifer thought. She wondered why both he and Jonathan seemed to presume that Meredith would lose.

Mark dropped onto the sofa between Derek and Jennifer after helping himself to a large glass of red wine from the table. They faced the fireplace from the sofa like the three monkeys. Jennifer wondered why Meredith had invited them on election night, knowing that she was going to be out. How long would they have to wait?

"Everyone knows about the attack on the old woman in the village, I presume?" said Derek.

They all adopted a solemn expression and nodded at each other. Emma was staring at her phone, as though willing it to ring.

"Terrible business," said Mark. "It's the talk of the village."

"Actually, Pippa knows all about it. She was the one who tipped off the police that it was her stepsons who drowned Didier, the wind farm protester," said Jennifer. "It seems the developers must have been behind it after all."

"Wow," said Derek. "And I thought that she was being beaten up over the succession."

"It seems that the attack on the stepmother was because they blamed her for denouncing them to the police," said Jennifer. "I hear she's back at home now, but the old woman's lost both of them, hasn't she? It's absolutely tragic."

"I heard that the killer was blind drunk when he stabbed her," said Jonathan.

"Wouldn't you have to be, to do something like that?" Jennifer gave him a cold stare. "He also told the police that the two of them hadn't intended to kill Didier, just intimidate him."

"Maybe they didn't realise how deep those slurry tanks are," said Derek.

"At least she's got the house now," Mark chipped in. He stood up in search of a refill while the others took another sip of their drinks.

Emma checked her watch before getting up again. She went into the kitchen to fetch some nibbles.

"It's not much," she said, coming back with plates piled high with finger sandwiches which she set down on the coffee table. They each took a napkin and were just helping themselves when Emma's phone rang.

They watched her listen before exclaiming, "That's fantastic! Well done!" Emma rang off and turned to look at them all. "She's won!" She shook her head in disbelief. "I don't think she expected to be elected in the first round. She's coming right over with Solenn."

They heard the doorbell ring again. "That must be Pippa," she said.

Pippa came in carrying a tray.

"Meredith's list has been elected in the first round!" Jennifer told her, as soon as she'd taken off her mac.

"Great! I knew that would happen," said Pippa, smiling. "That's what my customers were saying." She went round offering everyone a sausage roll, leaving the tray on the coffee table.

"These are excellent," said Mark, licking his lips.

Emma seemed unsure as to what to do next. "Should we wait till Mum gets here to crack open the champagne?" she asked.

"Of course not!" said Mark.

At that moment, they heard the front door. Meredith came in, teetering slightly as though about to lose her balance, followed by Solenn. Derek got up to help steady her before kissing his wife.

"Are you all right?" Derek asked Meredith. "Come and sit down."

He escorted her to the sofa and found another seat for himself next to Solenn. Meredith seemed to have forgotten their presence. "Oh my God, oh my God," she repeated. Then she began to cry. "If only Craig were here," she sobbed.

"Come on, Mum, this is what you wanted. Dad would be proud of you. Well done," Emma said, standing behind her. "I think we've got exactly what's needed at this point. Champagne! Let's celebrate!"

She went back into the kitchen in search of champagne glasses and bubbly. Meredith's eyes searched for Solenn.

"I can't believe this. I'm so sorry, everyone, for being late. What happens now?" she asked.

"Next week there will be a meeting, and the people on your list will decide who is to be mayor," said Solenn. "But as you were top of the list, that means you."

Meredith sat back in the sofa, fanning herself with one hand.

"By the way," said Solenn, "Mathieu is so unpopular in the village that I saw a lot of ballots where his name had been crossed out. Basically, your list won the majority of fifty per cent plus one and so you were all elected in the first round."

Jonathan raised a champagne glass. "Here's to our next mayor, Meredith Barton," he said. "*Avec Vous!*"

"*Avec Vous!*" everyone said, clinking their glasses and laughing.

Somebody's phone rang and the sound was traced to the sofa. Meredith answered and spoke in French. Her face was serious. Was it bad news? She said, "Thank you for ringing," and ended the call.

"That was Mathieu . . ." she said. "He phoned to congratulate me."

"Wow!" Pippa exclaimed.

"So Louennec has got its first English mayor," said Jennifer. "That's huge."

"Maybe they like us after all," said Jonathan, grinning.

CHAPTER 49: THE ATTIC

In the days that followed the official announcement of her election, Meredith's phone never stopped ringing.

On the plus side, she managed to stop Sylvie Le Goff from calling her Marie once and for all. But her time was no longer her own.

The *Daily Telegraph* lost no time before contacting her. The Paris correspondent who had interviewed her arrived after a six-hour drive with a photographer. They made sure she was photographed talking to a dairy farmer with his herd because "that strikes a chord with our readers".

"I thought your readers were mostly dead," she said. "At least that's what my late husband used to say. He was a journalist by the way. But don't put that in your piece."

A couple of days later the article appeared under the headline: "Englishwoman beats French mayor after wind farm battle".

"I told him more than once that I'm *French*," she complained to Pippa in the bakery when she picked up her baguette. Pippa raised her eyes to heaven as though saying, "God save us from these journalists."

"It's good publicity though," said Pippa. "For you and for Louennec. It's put the village on the map."

"Yes. I was telling the reporter about the *Vieilles Charrues* summer festival in Carhaix. He'd never heard of it, can you believe? Nearly 300,000 people at a rock festival in Brittany! I told him he needs to get out of Paris more."

"Good for you," said Pippa, moving to the till.

Jennifer came in as Meredith was popping her coins into the machine.

"Morning ladies," she said. "What's new, Meredith? Everything OK?"

Meredith turned to check that the three of them were alone in the bakery.

"Is Gwen here?" she asked in a conspiratorial whisper, pointing to the back room.

"Don't worry, she'll be here in half an hour," said Pippa. "What's up?"

"What's up is that one of Mathieu's deputies, Jean-Michel, told me something. He switched sides to join my list, remember? It was about the rumours that Mathieu had got a bribe from the wind farm developers."

"Yes but didn't we already know about that rumour?" said Pippa.

"Wait, what Jean-Michel told me is that Craig found out about a payment and confronted Mathieu about it — only days before he died! He heard Craig shouting in the corridor to Mathieu after a council meeting. So that means that Mathieu had a motive for getting rid of Craig!"

"Gosh," said Jennifer. "Did Jean-Michel tell the police?"

"I asked him," said Meredith, "and he said that he hadn't mentioned it because he didn't think about the connection until the election campaign. I think that's why he approached me about joining my list. But I don't know why he sat on this information until now. Maybe he didn't want to say anything as long as Mathieu was mayor."

"Maybe Jean-Michel thought he'd be next," said Pippa. "Seriously. Anyway, he ought to talk to the police," she went on. "He's one of my customers. I'll have a word with Yann tonight. But do you think that Craig might have had any proof when he challenged Mathieu? Like the bank transfer or something?"

"That's a good idea," said Meredith. "I've still not gone through all Craig's papers in the attic. To be honest, I couldn't face it."

"Do you want me to help you?" Jennifer asked.

"No, I'll have to do it."

Another customer came in and their conversation ended.

"Keep us posted then," said Pippa.

* * *

Meredith pulled down the stepladder leading to the attic, and threw open the door. She climbed to the top of the ladder and, twisting uncomfortably, managed to hoist herself inside. From a sitting position she was able to stand up almost straight.

She'd never liked venturing into the loft, which had always been Craig's job. She'd only been up once in the months since his death, to store his things. She'd allowed Captain into the house while she searched, and he was sitting obediently on the landing which somehow reassured her.

She regretted now that, apart from putting in insulation and a chipboard floor, they'd never taken the trouble to install lighting in the attic which stretched along the full length of the house. Meredith switched on the torch on her phone to search the cardboard boxes piled high. What skeletons lurked in here?

The room felt musty. Long spiders' webs were draped from the wooden rafters over discarded items of furniture. Craig's old clothes were folded inside plastic containers which were in one of the corners. She still hadn't had the courage to sort them out and either throw them away or donate them to charity.

Then she spotted what she was looking for at the far end of the attic and made her way there, bent double under the eaves. Craig had marked each box with the year in felt-tip pen. She'd pulled out the file about the wind farm campaign earlier from a box on top of a pile, and she picked it up again. It was heavy and fell from her hands onto the floor, spilling its contents.

The dog barked, hearing the noise.

"Shut up, Captain!" Meredith swore out loud and cleared a space for herself to sit on the floor. She'd put on some old tracksuit bottoms that she used for gardening to avoid getting dust on her proper clothes. One by one, she checked the files which contained the past year's council minutes and other sheets of paper, some in Craig's untidy handwriting.

Her eyes began to feel strained from reading by the light of her phone. She wondered whether to phone Emma for help in taking the box downstairs for further investigation. But after an hour she realised her search for evidence was in vain.

She began to cry, the tears streaming down her face. They were tears of grief, self-pity and disappointment. She rubbed her eyes on her jumper sleeve and said out loud to the spirit of Craig, "Why did you do this to me?"

CHAPTER 50: SUSPECTS

"So that's it, then," said Pippa. "We're back to square one."

She and Jennifer were seated at her kitchen table with a notebook in front of them. Pippa had scribbled down the timeline of the murders and sabotage in the village and crossed out suspects one by one. She put a big cross through the name of Mathieu.

"I'm not surprised that Meredith couldn't find any hard evidence like a bank transfer. When I mentioned it to Yann, he was adamant that the mayor wouldn't risk getting involved in taking a backhander."

"Bugger," said Jennifer. "No motive, then."

"Shall we have a drink? You don't have to rush off, do you?"

"No, that's fine. The kids and Jonathan have all gone away for the long weekend. It's a blessed relief, actually. I feel like I'm walking on egg shells all the time, when Jonathan's in the house. Some days I wish he'd go away and never come back. But the children need him."

"Are you arguing all the time though?" asked Pippa.

"No. Not anymore. I guess it's like a truce in a war. We're polite to each other, just about. But the question is whether we have to put on this face until the children have finished school? I'm not sure I can manage years more of that."

"And do you think he's given up Emma?"

"Honestly? I've no idea. Maybe Meredith knows, but I'm not going to ask her. Thanks."

Pippa had poured them both a glass of Gros Plant from her fridge and they clinked.

"We must be missing something," said Pippa. She pointed at the notebook.

"Did we rule out anyone from the Louennec players? A fellow Brit? I'm not sure we ever went through everyone who was there at the dress rehearsal," said Jennifer. "I mean, when I think back to that video, I couldn't see Mark at the back. He was sitting with us until the halfway point unless he was on stage."

"I think he may have gone to the loo," said Pippa.

"That's not a crime, is it?" said Jennifer. "But I don't remember him being there when the police arrived and started questioning everybody. So that would mean he didn't come back."

"So what?" said Pippa.

"Wait — what if he'd hidden the murder weapon and then picked it up and went off with it!"

"It's possible I suppose . . . But a bit far-fetched, surely?"

They both took another sip of their wine. Pippa produced some homemade cheese straws and they chewed while they ruminated.

"OK," she said. "We have to do this systematically. Are we presuming that Meredith didn't kill Craig? And that you and I didn't murder him?"

"Correct," said Jennifer, laughing. "And Jonathan too . . . maybe. Although he was holding a rifle!"

"Solenn? I think we can rule her out too."

"Unless she was the instrument of a French person — such as Mathieu!"

"I like that theory. An undercover agent," said Pippa. She wrote down Solenn's name and circled it. "But what about Derek then? I mean he's well integrated into the community. He and Craig might have had a vendetta we didn't know about."

"Pippa, don't be ridiculous. He was by the stage. We need to focus on people at the back. Remember it was someone that Craig knew, it was a person he recognised in the moment before he was shot."

Pippa looked down at her notebook again and took a long swig of wine.

"That leaves Emma. Would she kill her own father?"

"Ha!" said Jennifer. "I wouldn't put anything past that woman."

"Are you serious?"

"Well, no. Not really."

"So that only leaves one person. And that person is Mark."

CHAPTER 51: IN VINO VERITAS

"If I have any more of your wine, I won't be able to drive home," said Jennifer.

"In vino veritas," said Pippa. She was thinking back to her only proper conversation with Mark, at the café-tabac. "Did I tell you that Mark's wife killed herself?"

"Oh no! The poor thing," said Jennifer. "I wish I'd known. I've hardly ever spoken to him."

"Yes. It made him seem more sympathetic, actually. In fact, I thought that it was probably why he hit the bottle so much."

"Of course. Did he say anything else?"

Pippa racked her brains to remember their conversation. Then she grabbed Jennifer's wrist.

"Oh, do you know what he said? He told me that he's going back to England. Isn't that a bit of a coincidence?"

"Could be, I suppose," said Jennifer. She leaned in and clinked Pippa's glass. "I've got to go," she said, standing up rather unsteadily.

"One sec, Jennifer. We've just decided he's the main suspect. So, assuming he's still living in the village, we'll have to go to his place when he's out, and see whether he's stashed the murder weapon somewhere."

"Are you mad?" said Jennifer. "How do we know when he's out?"

"Easy. Because, regular as clockwork, he goes to the bar-tabac. He's there for a drink every evening."

* * *

Pippa and Jennifer walked to the house on the edge of Louennec which resembled so many of the traditional two-bedroom homes in the village, standing directly on the street. Straggly hollyhocks framed the front door which had shuttered windows on either side. The curtains were drawn even though it was still daylight.

Mark's car was parked at the side. Pippa beckoned to Jennifer. Obviously, they were going round the back.

All was quiet. There was no sound from a dog inside. The blue paint was peeling on the back door which had two glass window panes. If anyone was there they would be seen. Pippa knocked and listened. Then she twisted the back door-knob and pushed.

"Damn," she said. "Why doesn't he leave the door open like everyone else?"

"What are you talking about? Nobody in the village leaves their door open these days . . . come on, I reckon we've only got about half an hour before he gets back."

"What about the kitchen window, then?"

"But how can we get in without smashing it?" Jennifer replied.

"Try the next room along?"

They went along the back wall where the toilet's frosted window was ajar.

"Are you expecting me to get through that?" said Pippa.

They giggled.

"So much for sleuthing. This is ridiculous," Jennifer said.

"What if . . . ?" said Pippa. She began feeling in potted plants which stood on each side of the kitchen door. "He must have a plan B. I mean, for when he comes back sloshed and can't find his keys."

Jennifer lifted a pot of geraniums and looked underneath.

"Phew," she said, holding up a key on a chain. But it didn't fit in the lock.

They ran round to the front, making sure that there were no passers-by who would betray them. What if Derek turned up on his daily run?

The key slid into the lock like oil. The door swung open, and they shut it quickly behind them. They were standing in the hall which had doors leading into a room on either side. At the end was the kitchen, where the stone sink was piled high with washing-up. *Note to self, always do the washing-up before leaving home*, thought Jennifer. She remembered her granny reminding her to wear clean knickers in case she was run over.

Pippa pointed, as though indicating that she would take downstairs, and Jennifer the upper floor.

"Pippa, why are you doing that? You're making me nervous. We know he's out so just be normal!"

"Shall we both go up, then? If it were me, I'd hide the gun under the bed."

"Too obvious." Jennifer was already climbing the narrow wooden staircase. A bedroom door was open. The bed was unmade in the airless room which had a vague smell of unwashed armpits.

Jennifer wrinkled her nose. "This is the man cave," she said, resisting the temptation to open a window.

Pippa got onto her knees to look under the bed, and began coughing.

"There's so much dust." She stood up. "I don't think he's hoovered under that bed for years."

They searched through the wardrobe, opening shoe boxes and searching the pockets of shabby cardigans and two jackets hanging inside.

Jennifer shook her head. "Let's try the other room."

Pippa went into the bathroom and checked the mirrored cabinet over the washbasin.

"Oh God, too much information," she said. "Mark is on all sorts of pills."

"He could stop drinking if he wants a healthier life," Jennifer commented. "Come on, we've not got much time. What if he comes back while we're up here?"

"Look at this." Pippa had opened the cabinet's bottom door. "He's got gallons of mouthwash in here!"

The second bedroom was smaller, and arranged into a study. Mark's laptop was on the desk. Jennifer rifled through the drawers which contained nothing but files.

They made for the stairs. Halfway down, Pippa froze.

"Did you hear that?" she said.

"What?" Jennifer whispered.

"That noise. Like rattling. What if he's back?"

"Stop it, you're scaring me!" said Jennifer. "I'm not sure this was a good idea. Let's get downstairs and check there. Quickly."

They went into the small living room.

"Do you think we dare open the curtains?" Jennifer asked.

"No. Let's switch on the light."

The sideboard drawers overflowed with cutlery and dining room mats. Two were reserved for a collection of beer mats.

Pippa turned round. Their search was becoming increasingly desperate. "Look, there's a drawer in the coffee table!" she cried out, pulling it open. It was empty.

"Look," said Jennifer. "Maybe we've got it wrong. Or maybe we're right and he chucked away the gun on the night of the murder. I think we should go."

They stood in the centre of the room and cast their eyes into every corner. Jennifer picked up the cushions from the sofa and peered underneath. She shook her head.

They crossed the hall into the dining room and switched on the light. The room was furnished with four wooden chairs and a cheap table. The patterned wallpaper, stained by traces of damp, had clearly not been replaced for years.

"I can see why Mark never had us over for a panto rehearsal," said Jennifer. "It's not exactly inviting in here."

"Focus, Jennifer. What about looking under the rug? I've seen them do that in crime dramas on TV."

The two of them shifted the dining table and rolled up the rug underneath. One of the planks of the parquet floor appeared to be loose.

Pippa held up her hand as though consigning the operation to silence. Jennifer could hardly restrain herself from laughing. Pippa was back on her knees, stretching out her arm into the hole underneath.

"Can you go further along?" said Jennifer.

At that moment they heard the front door open. They looked at each other in horror.

Pippa raised a finger to her lips. Her other arm was still reaching under the floorboard and her bottom was sticking into the air. Jennifer searched the room in vain for a hiding place.

They heard Mark's heavy footsteps on the wooden floor. The door opened. The dining room light was shining on the two women like a prison floodlight.

"What the hell are you two doing here?" he said.

CHAPTER 52: THE TRUTH AND NOTHING BUT . . .

Pippa pulled out the steel object whose tip she had felt under the floorboard.

"Mark, it's over," she said, getting to her feet. She held up the handgun like a trophy. "We know you did it. Just tell us why."

Jennifer was impressed by her preternatural calm.

But Mark hit back aggressively. "You don't know anything about grief, do you?"

What was he talking about? Pippa seemed to sense he needed to get something off his chest.

"Why don't we sit down?" Pippa said, gently. "Are you talking about your wife?"

Mark sat, or collapsed, onto a chair and gestured that they make themselves comfortable. They drew up two chairs and sat side by side. Pippa placed the gun on the table, within reach. A long moment passed while Mark composed himself, his face contorted with the pain of a memory.

"It was more than ten years ago," he said, almost to himself. Then looking straight at Pippa he said, "But the hurt never goes away. Not even now. I still think about Jill every day."

"I'm so sorry, Mark," said Jennifer. "But can you tell us what happened between you and Craig? I'm afraid I can't see the connection between your wife dying and you deciding to kill him . . ."

"Yes, tell us from the beginning," Pippa suggested. "Did you know Craig from before, when you were in England?"

"Not personally, no. But I knew of him. Because he was the reporter who made a mistake in a story about my wife's company. As a result of a single mistake in an interview with her, which the paper took too long to correct, her business collapsed. That sent her into a tailspin of depression and led to her suicide."

He sighed. "That's it in a nutshell."

"And so you blamed Craig for her death?"

"Of course I did!" he said, glaring at Jennifer. "So unprofessional and reckless."

He got up and went to a sideboard where he took out a bottle of whisky. He held it up as though offering them a glass. They both declined and watched him serve himself a large one.

"What was her company?" Jennifer asked.

"It was a fashion retail site, called Frocksanstuff, where Jill was one of the founders. She was at a capital markets day event where she saw Craig and after his report came out the stocks fell off a cliff . . ." His voice trailed off.

"Oh no! Your wife was Jill Riley? I think I met her once, at a women's networking event," Pippa exclaimed.

At the mention of his late wife's name, Mark jolted upright as though injected with an adrenalin shot. He stared at Pippa in astonishment.

"Yes. I worked in the City at the time. I'm pretty sure she was talking about Frocksanstuff. I remember she started out with a clothes boutique, didn't she? It was in the papers when she died."

Mark nodded slowly. "Yes. She kept her maiden name. So Craig never knew about the connection with me."

Jennifer leaned forward. "Go on," she urged.

"Anyway, Craig was eventually sacked from that job for being cavalier with the truth. Not a good thing for a business reporter," he said with a sardonic grin.

"And did you follow him when they moved to Somerset?"

"No. I bided my time. In fact I didn't think of revenge at first. The idea came to me later. When I googled him and discovered that he'd turned up in Louennec, I thought I'd do the same. I needed a change myself, and was bored with my job."

"And you saw your chance to get even in Mother Goose?" said Pippa.

"That's right. It was a lucky break, I suppose."

"Not for Craig though," said Jennifer, glancing at Pippa.

"That man deserved to die. He killed my wife!"

"What if it was an innocent mistake?" said Jennifer.

"Innocent mistake my arse!"

The three of them sat in silence for a moment, each nursing their thoughts. Jennifer said, "Tell us about the evening of the dress rehearsal. I remember you going out to the loo in the break."

He nodded. "Yes. I'd hidden the gun in the Gents. I stood at the back and waited for the cue, then fired it and went straight home. I couldn't take the risk that the cops would come and find me with the weapon."

"The cue. You mean 'He's behind you'?"

"Of course."

Jennifer leaned forward and spoke to him urgently. "But Mark, you know you can't run away, don't you? You've got to hand yourself in."

He almost seemed relieved. His eyes were glazed. He took a long swig of his drink and said, "I know."

Pippa pushed her chair back and went out of the room. They heard her on the phone in the hall having a brief conversation with someone before coming back to the dining room.

"I've just given Yann the address. He's coming over now," she said to Pippa. "He's a gendarme," she added, for Mark's benefit.

He remained slumped in his chair and gestured at the gun.

"That thing's not loaded, by the way," he said.

CHAPTER 53: THE SHOW MUST GO ON

It was the second week of July and a heatwave had settled over Louennec. The temperatures were rising and so were the villagers' tempers. In this part of France, they could cope with torrential rain and gusting winds, but not extreme heat.

Brittany was on "red alert" with record temperatures which were twenty degrees higher than normal. For Pippa, that meant that in the bakery's back room, the heat was unbearable. She was counting the days to August when they'd close for a month.

She walked slowly home at 7.30 p.m. after prepping her batches for the next morning's bake, and took a quick shower before changing into a flowing cotton dress. It was suffocating outside. For the past three days, she'd kept the curtains and shutters closed like they do in southern Europe. Nobody she knew in Louennec had air conditioning.

She heard the doorbell ring and picked up her handbag. Yann was waiting outside.

"Are you ready?"

* * *

Jennifer and Jonathan held open the car doors waiting for the children to pile in.

"Where's Mariam?" Jennifer asked Luke who emerged from the front door, leaving it open.

He pulled his earbuds out of his ear.

"What?"

"Here she comes," said Jonathan. "I suppose this is the fashion on the Riviera these days."

Their daughter's hair was loose and she'd sprinkled glitter on her cheeks. She was wearing a black T-shirt over a short skirt and running shoes. The T-shirt spelled out *Arctic Monkeys* on the front.

"At least she'll be able to run away, if anyone bothers her," Jennifer said to Jonathan. "Get in," she said, rather abruptly, to Mariam.

They drove through the parched fields on their way to the *Vieilles Charrues*.

"Look at that," said Jennifer, gesturing towards a desiccated maize field. "One of the dairy farmers told me his cows are stressed out from the heat."

"It's amazing they've not been out dumping manure in the streets in protest."

"That's not fair," she said. "Look at our vegetable patch. We'll be lucky if we get any decent carrots and onions this year."

"Of course we will. Guess who's been watering them?"

"Didn't anyone tell you that you're not supposed to water them during the day?" said Mariam from the back seat. "You do know that this is the hottest summer ever in Brittany, and that it's going to get worse because of global warming? And all you're worried about is a stupid wind farm."

Luke immediately accused her of being a know-all, she retorted that he was a know-nothing and began pummelling his bare knees, which prompted him to pinch her arms.

"Stop it, you two!" cried Jennifer. "Behave."

Jonathan grimaced. He brought the car to a halt outside a small house on a leafy lane and Luke jumped out. They waited until the front door opened and he disappeared inside with a wave. With the windows rolled down they could hear loud rock music as soon as they turned onto the main road into Carhaix.

"Where are you meeting Pervenche?" Jennifer asked Mariam. Pervenche's father had come through with the promised free tickets to the concert but Jennifer now regretted not having bought some for themselves. She wondered whether the two girls would appreciate the band as much as she and Jonathan would.

"At the post office," said Mariam.

They looked up at the imposing gothic tower of the church as they neared the town centre. Jonathan dropped her by the marketplace so she could walk up to the post office square.

"Be good," he called out through the window as she slammed the door without a word.

"Have fun, see you tomorrow," said Jennifer to her back.

"Good grief, how many more years of this?" Jonathan groaned. "Does she think she's Greta Thunberg, or what?"

"Well, I don't blame her for being anxious. I mean, kids her age are going to be the worst affected by climate change, aren't they?" said Jennifer. "But at least she seems more comfortable in herself now, don't you think?"

"If you say so. Wait till she decides she's a vegan."

They crawled along behind a line of cars and found a parking space in one of the festival's designated fields, a long way from the action.

"Where are we meeting the others?" he asked, getting out of the car with their entry tickets.

"We can find a bar in the field behind the cinema. Let me look on my phone." They trudged along in the crowd until eventually Jennifer said, "There's Pippa and Yann."

She waved. The two of them were standing by a wooden picnic bench where three young people in shorts and T-shirts were sitting finishing their beers. Jennifer presumed that the two women were Pippa's student daughters. They made their way through a throng of young people to join them.

Pippa introduced them to her daughters and one of their boyfriends.

"They're camping." She had to shout over the sound of the pulsating rock music from a nearby stage.

"And how's it going?" Jennifer asked.

"Great," said one of them.

"So, drinks, anyone?" asked Jonathan. Pippa's daughters said they were heading off so declined. By the time Jonathan came back with beers they'd already gone, and they took their seats on the bench.

"The girls look like you," said Jennifer, raising her voice. "How long are they here for?"

"Just a few days," said Pippa. "They came for the festival and decided to camp because I don't have enough room for them at my place."

"You must be glad to have some time off," said Jennifer.

"Oh boy, yes. It will be my first real break since I opened."

"Are you going away?" Jonathan enquired.

"Yes, we're going to Corsica for a week, aren't we?" she said to Yann. "Then we'll see. I may go to Manchester, but nothing's decided yet.

"And Mariam's going down to the Riviera?" she asked Jennifer, who had recently described the situation on the domestic battlefield as "tense but calm".

"That's right. The parents of her friend Pervenche have a villa outside Nice."

"Lucky her."

Jennifer glanced in Jonathan's direction before adding, "And Jonathan may take Luke to England while I hold the fort here with Byron."

Meredith was the next to heave into view. She was a one-woman procession, advancing through the crowd like a member of the royal family, stopping to shake people's hands on her way.

"Hello everyone. I've just seen Derek and Solenn, I think they're coming to join us," she said. "Isn't it hot?"

Pippa made room for her on the bench, and she sat down heavily, fanning herself with one hand.

"Hello *Madame la maire*," said Jennifer. "How are you coping?"

"*Bonjour* Yann," she said, ignoring the others. Ever since Mark's arrest she'd made a point of making him feel welcome in their group. Yann acknowledged her greeting.

"What's the latest with Mark?" she asked him.

"He has a lawyer who is trying to persuade the judge to have him serve his sentence in the UK." He pulled down his mouth. "I don't think it will work, though. Maybe Peeper and Jennifer will have to intervene," he added with a smile.

They all laughed.

"Did you see that we organised another vote in the council about the wind farm project?" said Meredith. "And it passed unanimously this time. I'm not going to let it drop, now. I'll go all the way to the courts, if we have to."

"I bet the terrifying Madame Le Goff might have something to say about that," said Pippa.

"Oh." Meredith waved a hand as though batting away an insect. "I think her bark is worse than her bite, actually. I don't know why I was so scared of her. But my strategy is to hook up with other *communes* because we'll have a bigger voice that way. More of them round here are getting up petitions and the like to stop the march of the turbines.

"By the way," she went on. "I've been thinking. What would you say to doing a pantomime this Christmas? I don't want the whole thing to be jinxed just because of what happened the last time."

"That's a great idea," said Pippa. "Can I play the animal lead again?"

"And can I do the adaptation?" Jennifer asked.

"I don't see why not. I've got a lot of work on. If you want me to direct, we could have our first meeting after the holidays. Have you got something in mind?"

Jennifer smiled.

"Aladdin," she said straight away.

THE END

ACKNOWLEDGEMENTS

Two impressive women inspired this new series set in Brittany and I'm so grateful for them sharing their time and experiences with me. My sister-in-law, Brigitte Vallée, has coped with the challenges of a smallholding in rural Brittany for many years while also serving as a council member of her *commune*. My friend Céline Tran, who did a mid-career change from being a lawyer to retraining as a baker, swapped one kind of dough for another. Her fantastic little Paris bakery and café, BAKE, became an instant success and sells bagels to the French (among other delicious items).

I must also thank my faithful group of critical readers who gave me much-needed feedback and input on early drafts. They are, in alphabetical order: Nicholas Blincoe, Meg Bortin, Margaret Crompton, Mary Friel, Mike Gray, Charles Kaye and Rosemary Unsworth.

Last, but not least, I'm grateful, as ever, to my eagle-eyed editors at Joffe Books. Any mistakes, of course are mine alone.

THE JOFFE BOOKS STORY

We began in 2014 when Jasper agreed to publish his mum's much-rejected romance novel and it became a bestseller.

Since then we've grown into the largest independent publisher in the UK. We're extremely proud to publish some of the very best writers in the world, including Joy Ellis, Faith Martin, Caro Ramsay, Helen Forrester, Simon Brett and Robert Goddard. Everyone at Joffe Books loves reading and we never forget that it all begins with the magic of an author telling a story.

We are proud to publish talented first-time authors, as well as established writers whose books we love introducing to a new generation of readers.

We won Trade Publisher of the Year at the Independent Publishing Awards in 2023. We have been shortlisted for Independent Publisher of the Year at the British Book Awards for the last four years, and were shortlisted for the Diversity and Inclusivity Award at the 2022 Independent Publishing Awards. In 2023 we were shortlisted for Publisher of the Year at the RNA Industry Awards.

We built this company with your help, and we love to hear from you, so please email us about absolutely anything bookish at feedback@joffebooks.com

If you want to receive free books every Friday and hear about all our new releases, join our mailing list: www.joffebooks.com/contact

And when you tell your friends about us, just remember: it's pronounced Joffe as in coffee or toffee!

ALSO BY ANNE PENKETH

THE BRITTANY MURDER MYSTERIES
Book 1: THE BRITTANY MURDERS

DI CLAYTON MYSTERIES
Book 1: MURDER ON THE MARSH
Book 2: THE BAD SISTER
Book 3: PLAY DEAD
Book 4: MURDER AT THE MANOR